HOLDING MYSELF

VICTORIA J. BROWN

Print ISBN 978-1-912175-38-3

Simon, Alexia and Gabriella – my biggest fans.
Love you always
xxx

Prologue

The laughter was the strongest memory of that afternoon. We giggled as we ran through the perfectly trimmed hedges of the maze while Mum and Dad followed our screams of excitement. This type of frolicking would usually have had me, a twelve-year-old, sitting on a bench, far too cool to join in such childishness. There was something about knowing I wouldn't bump into my school friends, and my parents' enjoyment, that made the whole day different. I was relishing the fact that I was still a child. Libby was only six years old at the time, and pleasurably held my hand as we meandered round the densely grown hedges.

Mum had packed a bundle of sandwiches. We devoured our way through the mixture of ham, cheese and jam, picking at the plain-flavoured crisps, the pink, decorated cakes and the chocolate biscuits. The large red blanket allowed space for us all as we soaked up the glorious weather, appreciating the small breeze that cooled our clammy bodies.

Lampford Hall stood proudly at the top of the park but the Hall itself was not open to visitors. Lord and Lady Lampford had opened their delightful grounds to the public but wanted to keep their home private. A dwarf stone wall with wrought-iron railings separated the Hall from the gardens and three members of staff circled the magnificent place. The sandstone building gleamed elegantly in the sun as people stood outside the guarded area, taking photos which would allow them to savour the moment forever.

We had listened to Mum tell a story about the fairies who lived in the magical Hall (for Libby's benefit, not mine, although

I loved listening to her tales). Libby had been mesmerised as Mum told her they all have their own responsibilities. Libby, who'd lost her first tooth the month before, concluded that the 'tooth fairy' must have the most important job. Mum explained we couldn't go inside the magical Hall because if we saw the fairies the magic would disappear; just like we couldn't see Santa. I remember thinking that when I had children I'd want Mum to tell these amazing stories. She'd had them stored, adapting them for different scenarios. When I listened that day I wished I was younger, still believing in the magical spirit of childhood. It was a deep-rooted feeling. One that had nested with me since my discovery that Santa didn't exist (all because of Hannah Johnson, who hit me and told me I was stupid for believing such a ridiculous story). When Mum explained the truth, it wasn't only Santa that disappeared; the enchantment of childhood and that special ability to believe in anything also vanished.

Choosing to immerse myself in the childhood atmosphere of Lampford Park, I joined Libby on the swings, slides and roundabout. We fed bread to the ducks, carrots to the deer and lettuce to the rabbits. We devoured soft chocolate ice-cream which trickled with chocolate sauce, chocolate sprinkles and a chocolate flake absolute luxury. We ran through the water fountains, tasting the splashes that bounced against our skin. Our clothes were soaked right through. Mum and Dad watched us from the edge, their arms linked together, enjoying our squeals of exhilaration. Over-excitement unleashed our deviant side as we dragged Dad by the arms, pulling him into the water jets. Libby and I laughed hysterically as he chased us through the shower of cold, refreshing water.

On the journey home, we all (except Mum) had to take off our clothes. Libby and I were down to our pants. Poor Dad had to strip off too: his shirt and trousers were soaking wet. Mum wrapped me and Libby tightly in blankets as fatigue engulfed us. I remember closing my eyes as they joked about hoping they didn't have an accident or get pulled by the police.

'What would they think?' Mum laughed.

It was decided that fish and chips would end the day nicely. Mum dropped us off at home with strict instructions to get our pyjamas on, ready for a cosy and warm night. It was mine and Libby's job to rummage through our collection of videos and pick a suitable film for us all. It was always one of the Disney collection which Libby decided upon.

Usually Dad would have done the fish-and-chip run, but because we'd well and truly drenched him, Mum insisted she go. I still wonder to this day: if we hadn't soaked him, would she still be here?

I wanted to ask the policeman that, as he sat with Dad in the lounge, relaying the news that Mum had been involved in a car accident.

She didn't make the fish and chip shop.

She died.

Instantly, they said.

1

'I think I'm pregnant.'

'What!'

'I know.'

'You think?' Suzy smiled. 'So, you might not be.'

'You're right, I might not be, but I'm four days late.'

'That's nothing. Sometimes I'm a week late.' Optimism shone from her eyes, her gentleness always present as she relaxed back in her chair.

'I'm never late and I feel so ill.'

'You wouldn't be ill after four days, would you?'

'Some of my customers say they knew as soon as it happened.'

'Really?'

I nodded, raising my eyes at the absurdity that a woman would know when one of her eggs had been impregnated. With flashes of how and when it could have happened piercing through my mind, I asked, 'Can you remember that ball I went to with Max?'

'God, how could I forget?' Suzy groaned and we both laughed at the memory of me dragging her around Newcastle, York and Leeds, looking for the perfect dress. Suzy had commented that she didn't want to get married, due to the amount of time it had taken to buy that dress. So, let's not mention the shoes. I was so nervous about meeting Max's work colleagues for the first time. I wanted them to be impressed, or I didn't want Max to be embarrassed; I wasn't sure which was the more important. I knew I had to look my best: a scruffy beauty therapist is never a good advert. We'd shopped for weeks on end, but it was worth it: Max commented, as did most of his colleagues, about how stunning I looked. It didn't stop the nerves, though.

'Well, remember I told you I was that nervous, I drank too much and threw up in the toilets before the meal was served?'

'I still can't believe Max doesn't know about that.' Suzy laughed. Then suddenly, her smile vanished. 'But that was, what? Seven, eight weeks ago? Did you miss last month's—'

'You remember a few weekends back we went to the Lakes?'

'Of course. It's when I met Michael,' she giggled, like a teenager.

'Anyway, I took two packs of pills back to back so I wouldn't have my period whilst we were away.'

'Good thinking.'

'Well, now I'm due on and four days later it's still not happening.'

'But, if you've taken two packs together this can delay it.' Suzy was a font of knowledge.

'I think so, but I don't think I'd be this late.' I ran my hand through my dark mane, the shine and texture inherited from Mum, the colour from Dad. 'Plus, I feel so sick, my boobs hurt, and they're bigger. I thought it was because I'd taken two packs of pills, but I know it's not.'

'You don't know for sure.'

'I'm sure enough - and I don't know what the hell to do about it.' Tears formed and I swallowed the lump in my throat.

'Have you talked to Max?'

'Not yet. There's no point saying anything if I'm not.' I sipped my coffee, trying to calm my nerves.

'Right, come on. Let's go.'

'Where to?'

'To buy a test.' Suzy was already out of her seat as I sat stubbornly in mine. Not only was my sofa the most comfortable place to be, I'd had the day from hell …

***

It was one of those days when I'd wished someone had warned me how hard it would be to run my own business. I'd opened the salon two years ago and, successful though it was, there was plenty of room to improve. But it was my baby. My dream, my soul, my everything – though that didn't stop cash-flow problems and tax returns. For the first time, I hadn't wanted to face the daily endurance, not because of the paperwork but because I felt so ill. I wished I had a boss and could call in sick. I couldn't face the customers, the smells or performing the treatments.

Melanie, my senior therapist, and I had organised the diary so I could come in late. A first; Melanie had been with me since day one, so she knew I was ill. Living above the salon was great, but usually I was in before everyone; therefore, none of the customers knew the secret door to my tranquil habitat. However, as I lay on my couch working myself up to venturing downstairs, I heard the raised voice of an unhappy customer. I wanted to cry, as I crawled on hands and knees towards the private door.

The taste of dustbins (or what I imagined dustbins to taste like if all the contents were blended together) swilled around my tongue, the bitterness burned the back of my throat from when I'd thrown up five minutes earlier. I could hear my bed calling me. But I couldn't let my customers down: they had appointments, they might not come back. Many of them demanded that I be their only therapist. Not because I was the best beauty therapist, but because I was the owner. It made them feel special. But this morning, for the first time, I'd divided a few treatments between the girls. Sophie, our trainee, had now qualified and was doing well, so I'd trusted her to perform a few treatments – but the commotion I could hear downstairs told me that something was obviously amiss.

'I'm not paying.' I recognised the voice. It was one of my best customers.

'Morning, Mrs Donnelly.' I entered from the back as if I'd been in one of the treatment rooms. My breathing was deep. I sounded as if I was trying to be sexy, when all I needed was more air in my lungs before I passed out.

'I'm not paying, Kathryn. I'm really not happy.' She turned on me and I caught Melanie looking anguished, as two other customers watched in anticipation. I'd refreshed my mouth with a mint, but my stomach was still churning. I held onto the reception desk, trying to disguise my inability to focus. The support helped me not to sway, as I tried to concentrate on smiling. Smile, then speak, I told myself. Speak she's waiting for you to speak. I could sense Melanie looking at me, begging me to handle this. Did they all think I was drunk? The young, just-married WAG, seemed oblivious to the state I was in. 'She's only gone an' taken it all off!' She pointed ferociously at Sophie, who cowered in the doorway, tears forming as she bit her lip.

I could see Melanie's cheeks and neck going blotchy with embarrassment. She knew I'd be wondering why Sophie had done Mrs D's treatment and not her.

Mrs D's already high eyebrows were raised. Her perfectly manicured hand rested dramatically on her hip as her stare burned through me. I decided to take her away from prying eyes. (I was also worried I might faint or be sick on her; can you imagine?) 'Shall we go out the back?'

'NO! You should have rearranged my appointment if you knew you couldn't make it this morning!'

'Please, Mrs Donnelly, it was an emergency,' I lied. 'I'm sorry this has—'

'*You're sorry?* I have no pubic hair left!'

Oh, bloody hell. I wanted to say we should be charging more for that treatment, but I thought better of it. 'Why don't you come and sit down?' I offered. 'How about a coffee?'

'I don't want coffee! I'm not paying.'

'That's perfectly fine,' I smiled, 'and for the inconvenience, your next treatment will be free.'

'I should think so.'

She calmed a little, though two free treatments were nothing compared to what she spent with us. She had at least two treatments a week. 'You've got to keep your man happy,' she would say. Her 'man' was Steve Donnelly, a top footballer who played somewhere important and was in the England team. (She dropped it into the conversation frequently.) All I really knew was, he wore red, was quite good-looking and had a well-shaped bum and legs. I knew the important stuff (we discussed him often when she'd left). Perhaps he didn't do Brazilians: maybe that's why she'd been so furious.

'You know how much business I bring your way, Kathryn. It would be a shame to lose that, wouldn't it?'

'Mrs Donnelly, I appreciate …' I couldn't finish my sentence. My body swayed. The salon began to rock, as if I were floating on a smooth river. My vision blurred into black haziness as I felt hands touching my shoulders and arms, the feeling of my body being moved.

'Kat, are you okay?'

'Get her some water.'

'Give her some space.'

Was I dreaming? I felt as if I'd been lifted from my body and pushed into oblivion. Slowly I brought my eyes into focus. Mrs D was looking horrified, which surprised me, because with the amount of Botox she'd had, she couldn't usually show much expression. Melanie was rubbing my back. She'd placed me on the chair behind our reception desk, concern etched across her face.

'I'm fine,' I managed, through the thickness of my dry mouth.

'Have some water,' Melanie demanded.

I did as I was told, breathing deeply, knowing I had to get through this. I couldn't show weakness to my customers; I couldn't let them see me like this. I was Kat, the one that was always together, the business-owner and beauty therapist, respected by all. I couldn't afford for this to get out. No-one could hear of this flaw in my perfected exterior. If Mrs D told her friends, it would mean so much business lost. This was not vanity, this was my livelihood.

'Honestly, everyone, I'm fine,' I lied, again. 'I skipped breakfast this morning and I've been up since five.' The latter not a lie.

'Breakfast is the most important meal of the day,' said Mrs D authoritatively. 'My Steve tells me all the time. He won't let me leave the house without my poached eggs on toast but sometimes

I won't eat anything else during the day. He'd kill me if he knew, but then, would he be happy without this figure to look at?' She spoke without taking a breath.

I was pleased that her self-absorption helped explain my illness. I was also satisfied that if this information got back to her friends I wouldn't be so badly looked upon. Missing meals in the world of Mrs D and her clique was a flaw they would probably admire.

After the drama had ended and Mrs D had filled us in on other items she and 'her Steve' had for breakfast, she left, thankfully, her Louis Vuitton bag swinging from her arm, her lips pursed and her Christian Louboutin extremely high heels clicking against the tiled floor. I actually felt sorry for her. Her jeans were so tight they looked painful. I was sure she'd have friction burns. Oh, poor woman. I felt her pain. Not that I have a hairless one, might I add. But that's not why I felt sorry for her. It was her insecurity; I wasn't sure she was that confident, self-assured person she presented. I could see myself in her. Following the laws of attraction, this would be the case: seeing something in those around us that is exactly like ourselves, but is something we don't want to see.

I looked at her made-up hair and face and considered her poised, self-assured manner. She was covering something; a weak, insecure core of emotion and self-doubt.

I knew the reason I pitied her. It was because I was like her. I showed the world a brave face, an outer layer of contentment.

But inside I was petrified.

2

'Right, I'm sure they put the tests in the medical aisle,' Suzy said.

I couldn't focus; the weight upon my shoulders was too heavy for me to carry. It was times like this, although nothing had been this drastic, I wished Mum was here. My poor mum, missed and loved to a point of desperation. I wished she was here to help me understand this great component that had been added to my life.

I would ask her, 'What shall I do?' I imagined she would cuddle me, like she would have done when I was twelve, and she would say, 'Whatever makes you happy.'

But this pregnancy didn't make me happy.

The supermarket was busy. Teenagers gathered in gangs outside, riding their bikes, loudly showing their presence; although not harmful, they were intimidating. Inside, women in suits, heels and other obvious work attire rushed around as children ran to keep up with them. People chatted in the aisle as if they hadn't seen each other for months. It became a community event, simply popping in for some shopping.

'I hope we don't bump into anyone,' I told Suzy as we wandered through the busy store.

'It'll be fine. We'll hide it.'

'How?'

'Watch!'

Our confident strides would have had no-one guessing what was going on in our lives. We headed for the clothes section. Well, Suzy did; I followed.

'What are we doing here?'

'Pick something we can hide the test with.'

'I'm not wasting money.'

'Well, buy something you'll wear again.' Suzy's tone was impatient as she rifled through some colourful shirts that were on offer.

'But I don't wear supermarket clothes.' I didn't mean to sound snobby, but I didn't.

'You don't know what you're missing. Look, here's a T-shirt is only £3.' She put it into my basket.

I took it back out again. 'I don't like it.'

'It's for the purpose of this mission!' Suzy was obviously enjoying this adventure, treating it like some kind of MI5 assignment.

I shook my head and breathed a sigh of desperation. I looked at the array of clothing, quite impressed there was so many nice things on offer. Finally, I picked up a loose black cardigan, visualising which tops and jeans it would suit. I wouldn't normally have bought it, but I wasn't wasting my money on something that would sit at the back of my wardrobe: I had enough of those. Putting it in the basket, we headed towards the aisle of medication. I kept my head down, but turning into the aisle, there was Mrs D. I pushed Suzy to carry on, but she was confused and she stopped. I bumped into her, sending her flying into a shelf of special offers.

'Ouch! Jesus, Kat, what are you doing?'

Her indignation caught not only Mrs D's attention but other shoppers too. So much for keeping a low profile! I looked quickly at the hair care, picking up a bottle of shampoo and conditioner, trying to look nonchalant. Shouting my name loudly with her squeaky irritating voice, Mrs D tottered towards us. Shit! I wished I'd worn a headscarf, big sunglasses and a wig. If she found out what I was doing, my news would travel around the whole of the North East before I'd had time to pee on the stick.

'Oh, my Lord!' Her loud exclamation made other shoppers stare. 'I've been so worried about you all day.'

'Oh, I'm fine.' I forced a smile.

'Over-worked,' she stated. That's not what she'd said this morning when she wanted free treatments.

'Well, perks of owning your own business.' Stupid thing to say, I know. I didn't know what else to say to her; I wanted to escape. She started chatting about a friend who'd died of a heart attack at the age of thirty. 'Stress-related, they'd said: he owned his own business.' People were looking; it was awful. I nodded, tried to stay focused as her mouth moved and sounds came out. She regaled us with another three stories before she said she had to dash.

'She's hard work,' Suzy commented. I was left feeling drained and nervous after the encounter. It would have been easier to just walk out of the shop. It was stressful enough trying to buy the kit, let alone use it. It was important that we looked natural, not dodgy, but our furtive peering and glancing made us look like untalented extras in a James Bond film.

'Just grab one,' I told Suzy. Grab it and run, I wanted to say. My phone rang loudly, startling us both. Clare's number flashed up. I wanted to leave it, but I knew she would ring again and again until I answered. She knew I wasn't at work, and God forbid I should have a life. As I walked away to answer it, Suzy held up her hands, mouthing, 'What are you doing?' She couldn't pick up a testing kit now without chasing me down the aisle, because I had the basket. It was meant to be a quick movement, grab the test, under the cardigan, then leave. I'd spoilt our not-so-well-thought-out plan.

'Are you free for dinner on Sunday?'

I didn't even get the chance to say hello. 'I'm not sure. I'll have to ask Max.'

'Well, I already have. He's free, so if you're free then it's sorted, yes?'

'Mmm ... yes.' I actually stuttered, as I often did when I spoke to Max's mother. She shocked me in ways I'd never realised possible. Why hadn't Max asked me what we were doing? She seemed to enjoy making me feel like we weren't a couple.

She made it so aware that he was *hers* first and foremost. She had the power to invite him to lunch without me. Perhaps I was meant to be grateful for being included. But I felt insulted by her, and betrayed by Max.

We said our goodbyes. I felt like calling Max and having it out with him. My nervous anxiety had turned to anger and resentment. Who the hell did she think she was? I could have screamed with frustration but I remembered I was actually trying *not* to draw attention to myself. My hand quickly grabbed a plastic box that contained a pregnancy test. I'd picked a more expensive one as I thought it would be more likely to tell me the truth, even though all the other tests showed just as high a percentage of accuracy.

'The cheaper ones are just as good,' Suzy said, as if reading my thoughts. 'They wouldn't be able to sell them otherwise.'

'I just grabbed it,' I said, not wanting to get into an argument.

The test was hidden under the superfluous cardigan as we headed out of the aisle. Task one was complete. Next, pay quietly, leave and hope no-one saw my special purchase. The queues were busy. People stood miserably, kids whinged, people talked, the tills beeped; I needed to be out. There was a queue for self-service and baskets but I couldn't do self-service because I'd need assistance to remove the security tag, which would take far too long. I wasn't sure why the security tag was necessary. Why would people steal pregnancy tests? I knew the answer, though: this was torture. I didn't want anyone to see me so it would have been easier to steal the test. I understood.

We stood quietly in the basket queue, checking for familiar faces every few seconds. I couldn't see Mrs D but I was worried she'd pounce on me as the security tag was being removed. Knowing she was in my presence sent waves of sickness through me. I was hot and flustered. I was incapable of thinking straight. Please hurry, I screamed inside.

Finally, it was my turn. I had a quick look around before handing the woman the kit from beneath the cardigan. I was so tempted to say, 'I don't need it now.' To my horror, she pressed her buzzer, shouted, 'James!' She asked him very loudly across the crowded shop to remove the tag from the pregnancy test. 'Sorry, love, mine doesn't work,' she said as she scanned the other accessories that I didn't need. My heart was in the pit of my stomach. The colour must have drained from my face.

Suzy was trying to stifle a giggle. 'It could only happen to you!'

A lump stuck in my throat. I was suffocating. Hot beads of sweat formed on my top lip and forehead as the heat raced through my body.

James brought back the test and released it from its plastic box. The woman scanned it, placed it in the carrier bag and then asked me for money, as casually as if I were buying milk, bread or butter.

We made it back home without any other interruptions. The shutters of the salon had closed out the world. I hated to see it so cold and uninviting; it didn't represent me or my business. Unlocking the door at the side of the building which led us up the stairs to my two-bed flat was very welcoming, though. Although the walls were bare brick, the photos and pictures I'd hung enhanced the entrance to my cosy abode. The flat was warm, but taking off my shoes I felt the coldness of the wooden floor on my toes.

'Come on,' Suzy chivvied me. Usually, I was the impatient one. I thought about how laid-back Libby would have been if she still lived with me. We wouldn't even have reached the shops. She'd moved out only a few weeks back. I think she needed some independence after living with her older sister for the past eight years. I didn't mind, but I did miss her.

'Okay, I'm doing it.' I unfolded the white sticks from their box, ripped off the plastic wrapping around one of the tests and read the instructions intently, ensuring no word was neglected.

'Just pee on the stick.'

'Okay, I'm going.'

I gracelessly hovered over the toilet, pleased no-one could see me. I was surprised at how my pee veered in different directions;

gross, I know. After washing my hands, that were unpleasantly wet, I went back to Suzy with the lid fitted back over the soaked, absorbent tip.

'Right! Put it over there and look away,' Suzy ordered. She read my confused expression. 'A watched pot and all that,' she said.

I caught sight of myself in the mirror which hung elegantly above my plush sofa. I stared at my pale complexion. My dark hair, usually full of bounce and vitality, looked drab and unkempt. Darkness had bordered my eyes over the last week, and my sickness had washed away the blushed, healthy glow I usually bore. I didn't recognise me. And I didn't feel like me either.

The thing is, I knew. Deep down I'd known for weeks, but I'd blocked it out and continued my daily dose of an oestrogen and a progestogen. I knew, not only because I was so sick, but because I was a tearful, tired, emotional wreck. I remembered the things that friends and customers had said about being pregnant. Like the fact I'd had a metallic taste in my mouth for the past few weeks and my sense of smell had increased twofold. I didn't normally have much sense of smell at all, but now I had a nose like a sniffer dog. Plus, I'd gone off my favourite perfume, which I absolutely loved. I had tried hard not to take any notice. I had tried so hard to block it out. Pretending it wasn't happening to me …

Picking up the test, I held it in my hand, like a precious piece of gold.

The pink cross was perfectly clear.

'It's a cross,' I told Suzy, as she quickly re-read the instructions in the hope that we'd misunderstood. But it confirmed what we already knew.

'Oh Jesus, Suzy, this is the worst thing that could happen.' My voice wavered as I spoke and the tears began to fall, drifting down each cheek and leaving a salty taste in my mouth. I looked at the stick that was about to change my life. How could this be possible? How could I have been so stupid?

Suzy brought me towards her for a cuddle. I took in her sweet smell; she always smelled of fresh flowers. Her blonde wisps brushed against my cheek as I took in the enormity of this conclusion.

How could I tell Max?

How could I tell him I was pregnant and I didn't want to be?

3

'Have you spoken to Dad?' I asked Libby. I actually meant Marianne rather than Dad. Dad never spoke to us on the phone, and he rarely had much to say when we went to visit. I still didn't like engaging Marianne into our lives, even though we were sixteen years on. So, I would call to speak to a man who didn't want to speak to me.

'I spoke to Marianne yesterday. They're okay, I think,' Libby yawned. Although I couldn't see her, I knew she would be lying down.

'I'm going to call in after we've been to Max's mother's for dinner.'

'God, rather you than me.'

'Stop it. Clare is a handful, but I'm sure it'll be fine. At least I'll get a proper dinner.'

'I'd rather starve.' Libby was never one to mince her words. The thing was she'd never actually met Clare, but she knew I thought Clare was against me.

'Anyway, how's this new job going?' Purposely, I changed the subject.

'Shit.'

'You can't leave another job! You've only been there a week.' I was lying on my cushioned sofa, waiting for Max to come and pick me up for the dreaded Sunday lunch.

'Kat, the people are wankers.'

'Libby, for God's sake you need to get a grip of your life.'

'I've got a grip of my life,' she retorted indignantly, as if it was everyone else who had the problem. 'The job is shite; the people are boring and the pay is crap.'

'Well, look for something else but don't leave that job. You're paying rent now, remember. You can't sponge off others like you do me.'

She went quiet as if I'd hit a nerve. I hated having a go at her, but sometimes she needed to be told. She was twenty-two going on two. She'd lived with me for eight years, finishing school, going to college then studying for her biological sciences degree. I was hoping she would follow in Mum's teaching footsteps, but when she graduated she decided she needed a job. She couldn't possibly study any more. I felt it was a waste, taking her knowledge and delivering it, not as a teacher, but as a barmaid and telephone salesperson. She'd never worked before that. I'd never forced her to either, believing if she put all her effort into her studies she could become the science teacher that Mum once was.

'Look, I've got to go. I'll speak to you later.' Libby hung up before I had time to say 'bye. I loved my sister; I felt responsible for her actions. But there was only so much I could do. I wanted her to have a nice life but Libby believed she already had a *fab* life. She was living it to the full. It was all this boring work stuff that got in the way. I knew she'd be off to the pub now, or they'd all be having some kind of house party. Her housemates were as unreliable as her; Calvin was an events manager who let them into all the clubs for free, and Josie was a creative, arty type, who sold her pictures on the internet, or something. She's so amazing, Libby would tell me, she's going to be massive. I would shake my head at her naivety. It wasn't so much the innocence but the fact that they lacked responsibility, the need to secure their future. Libby would argue that my superior self would get me nowhere in life.

Superior self?

Sometimes I wondered if she knew me at all.

As I clicked the phone off, Max texted to say he was on his way. I sent one back saying, 'Great, would it be okay to call in and see Dad on the way back?' His reply, 'Of course,' I was sure, was a cover for, 'Do we have to?'

***

The first time I'd introduced him to Dad, Dad had been rude and abrupt and we left after ten minutes. I hadn't wanted to tell Max about Dad's depression. There was a 50/50 chance that Dad would be in a good mood. Well, not singing and dancing, maybe, but making an effort to be sociable. But it didn't happen. I'd then had to explain to Max how Dad's depression had ruled our world; over-shadowed our lives. After his first (what the doctors termed) 'breakdown', which was the time he arrived home with Marianne, he never had any major episodes that needed him to be hospitalised. Sometimes he needed to rest and be alone. That wasn't a problem; I was quite happy to stay out of his way. He would have had worse attacks than the first if Marianne hadn't been there to calm him down (or drug him up) when she thought he was 'going on one'. When he had these horrendous moments, or episodes, he went eerily quiet, turned inward and became impossible to talk to. He would either ignore us or give us one-word answers that meant, 'Leave me alone'.

He would often shut himself away from us. He didn't leave the house much anyway, but when things were really bad he would confine himself to his bedroom. That always felt quite strange, because as the teenager, I was sure I was the one who was meant to lock myself away. Instead, I would leave the house, but I always took Libby with me. I hated leaving her in Marianne's clutches. I was responsible enough, though, to bring her back home at a reasonable time for bed. I'd never go out later with my own friends as I needed to know Libby was safe. I thought Marianne would brainwash her.

The crisis team had been our rock for the first couple of years. Sometimes they wouldn't hear from us in months, but frequently we would need their intervention for a while. Then all that stopped. I thought Marianne was filling them with lies, telling them everything was okay, so that she could take control.

Sometimes it wasn't his quietness that would penetrate throughout the house. As his solemnity turned to anger, it would seem like hours before the shouting and smashing stopped.

I realised now that the episodes probably only lasted twenty minutes, tops. This seemed endless at the time. It wasn't the depression that made him have these attacks. It was the drink. The depression ate away at him. I called them attacks, because it was as if he had been possessed. What I couldn't understand and never would, is why he put himself through it, why he drank so much, why he put himself in the position of feeling his life was uncontrollable. It made his world, and his life, sad. He couldn't seem to see this. He obviously thought he was blocking out his sadness; but he was magnifying it.

I've tried to imagine how he must have felt when he woke up in the mornings, filled with remorse, shame and the knowledge that the grief would start all over again. But he had Marianne. Maybe she had increased the intensity of his feelings for Mum, or the loss of her. I'm not sure; I'm not a counsellor. Well, only to my own clients, but not officially. I give my own opinions, like, 'You really need to sort him out,' or, 'Yes, I would get revenge.' If Dad were one of my clients, I would have been telling him he needed to get a grip, in the same way I tell Libby. Not that she listens. Dad probably wouldn't, either.

The truth is, I'd never tried to talk to him about it. He wasn't a client. He was my dad, who was usually unapproachable. I didn't try to stop his angry episodes. I didn't get involved in the shouting and screaming. We would let his aggression subside until he had no energy left, and more often than not he would collapse in the middle of the floor, sobbing uncontrollably. Marianne would kneel next to him with her hands on his shoulders and tell him it was okay. He would sob, 'I'm sorry,' in between, 'I can't do this,' and, 'I don't want to live.'

In the beginning, I used to push away the tears and whisper to myself, 'I miss Mum too, Dad.' But as I got older I started to lose patience, as well as sympathy. I don't think he wanted to help himself. He and Marianne wouldn't listen to me, so it was easier to stay out of the way. As I've said, I'm not quite sure why Marianne stayed, why she chose that life for herself. I often wondered what type of life she'd had before Dad. It couldn't have been good, or why would she stay with a man who was officially mentally ill and two children who showed her no respect? I couldn't connect with her, not only because she showed no self-respect in putting up with a life of endless misery, but because I felt resentful. She was trying to replace Mum and I couldn't let that happen. I knew she would push even harder if I had this baby. She would want to be a doting grandparent. But she wasn't a grandparent, and never would be a grandparent to my child. I couldn't allow that level of involvement. It would have been disrespecting Mum, trampling on her grave. I would explain to my child who Mum was. I would show them how special she was. I couldn't have Marianne swoop in and take her place.

This was just *one* of the reasons I couldn't have this baby.

***

'Hi, gorgeous.' Max wrapped me in his broad arms when he arrived and I felt the safeness of his presence, as I always did. And it was good of him to visit Dad and Marianne with me. Since that first, awful meeting he'd seen Dad's good side, many times, but the bad times soon outweighed the good. I loved him for supporting me.

'Missed you,' he added.

I told him I'd missed him too. I'd avoided him over the last three days. I thought if he could see my face, my emotional imbalance, he would guess. A barrier had been created, blocking me from telling him the truth, not because I didn't want to but because I didn't know what to do about the situation. Telling him should have been easy, but I was afraid it would make the whole event real. *I knew it was real*, but I suppose what I meant was I still had a choice what to do about it.

And I wasn't ready to make that choice yet.

4

Clare lived in Hutton Rudby, a small village close enough to the A19 but far away from the hustle and bustle of busy town life. We were surrounded by green and yellow fields as we took the country route. They represented a summer of daily sunbeams, but this hadn't actually been the case, we'd had haphazard bouts of rainfall, and we were still waiting for our official summer to arrive. Maybe it's here, I thought, as we enjoyed the atypical high temperature. The sun was shining. Max's convertible allowed us to breathe in the refreshing warm air. I enjoyed the gentle breeze on my face and felt more revitalised than I'd felt in a while.

When we arrived, I realised how quiet we'd been during our journey. Secretly, I was pleased. I hadn't wanted to talk.

He pulled into the gravelled entrance of his mother's sizeable home. The cottage style house stood two storeys high and looked welcoming with its covering of *Clematis Montana*. I only knew its name because when I first met Clare, I commented on the charming vine that surrounded her, 'Gorgeous home'. She'd soon put me right! It became apparent she was a very competent gardener.

Her eyes had looked down, her lips had tightened as she shook her head, as she'd said, 'It's *Clematis Montana*, dear.'

'Right sorry.'

'So, Maxwell tells me you live in a flat.' It had been a statement rather than a question.

I nodded, embarrassed by this critical inquisition.

'So, you don't possess a garden.'

'No, unfortunately not.' I'd smiled politely. I actually didn't see anything unfortunate about not having a garden; one less thing to up keep. Plus, I wasn't a fan of getting my hands dirty.

Max had laughed and said, 'Mother, Kat lives above her salon. It's great.'

'How ...' (she had searched for the right words) '... quaint.'

'You should book another appointment,' Max encouraged her.

'Oh yes, you should do that,' I found myself saying. *No, no you shouldn't*, is what I should have said, but I wanted to break through her insolence and be accepted into her family. I liked Max enough to make the effort for him. Six months later she still hadn't booked another appointment; her first being a gift from Max. Although pleased I didn't have to endure her in my work place I'd felt offended that my pride and joy was not good enough for her.

As we entered we were faced with an array of ornaments. Clare and Henry, Max's father, had travelled far and wide, and every country they'd visited was displayed within their home in some form. Not that I've travelled much, but if I'd acquired all the ornaments Clare had gathered, my home would have looked like a cross between an antique shop and car boot sale. Not Clare's home: everything had its rightful place.

We walked down the wooden hallway towards the double doors that opened into the magnificent kitchen, towards the sounds of Clare ordering Henry about.

'Henry, pour some wine dear,' she was saying as we entered. 'Oh, here they are.' Her eyes glowed when she saw Max. She cuddled him and kissed his cheek, as she gave me a small wave and asked if we wanted wine.

'I'm okay, thank you. I've not been too well.' I explained myself before anyone asked questions.

'I hope you're not bringing any germs with you,' Clare smiled, 'what with all those customers bringing in their ailments.'

Henry passed me some traditional lemonade. Its cloudy appearance felt appropriate for my mood. 'So son, how's the training going?' He patted Max on the back. They were both tall men, standing over six feet. Their broad shoulders added to their charisma. They were an influential force in anyone's company.

'Yeah, good,' Max said. 'I did a twenty-mile run yesterday and then a fifty-mile bike ride with Lawrence and Joe. We were knackered so we came back to the pub.'

'That's not good training,' I laughed, joining the conversation.

'Sounds like a good way to rest,' Clare piped up, not meeting my eye as she opened the oven to check the tenderness of the meat.

'It was Saturday. You know what Joe's like for his drink at the weekend,' Max said.

'I'm surprised he's as fit as he is,' Henry remarked.

'He got through the Ironman and two other triathlons last year. He did stop drinking for a while, but this is his first competition this year. I'm sure he'll stop drinking again soon. He knows what he's doing; he's training at least six hours every day,' Max said.

They were training for the Ironman Triathlon, a gruelling series of races that had to be completed in seventeen hours. A swim for 2.4 miles, on bikes for 112 miles and a marathon run for 26.2 miles. They only had about six weeks to train, but they'd done many before so they weren't deterred. Max was really excited about the contest and I admired him for his commitment and his tenacity. I couldn't think of anything worse. I couldn't comprehend even a one-mile run.

'You'll be fine, son.' Henry patted Max on his back again; a manly gesture that showed he was proud.

'How's work?' Clare asked him.

'Busy. We've signed this massive deal with some guys from America. We'll be developing shopping centres throughout England, but they'll have children's play facilities. Amazing, really.'

'Well done,' Henry said, obviously impressed. Max, on top of his extra activities, was an architect. It was his own firm; he'd started small but he was now winning huge contracts. He'd gone from employing two staff, to nineteen. On paper, he was a single-minded business tycoon making his way to the top. In reality, he was soft-natured with a good heart.

'Talking about friends being fit and doing really well,' Clare said as she rubbed her hands on a linen cloth, 'I saw Gina the other day. She is doing *so* well.'

Gina. Gina as in Max's ex-girlfriend. Why would Clare bring up Gina? Why would she associate the word 'fit' with an ex? I felt my heart beating a little faster. Her need to mock me was obvious. Well, to me, anyway.

'I bumped into her the other day. She said she's doing great, just been promoted,' Max added, as if they were talking about someone who wasn't as intrusive in our lives as she was.

'Wonderful, isn't it? Paula mentioned it. She'll be running that hospital soon.' Clare laughed at her own not-so-funny joke.

I kept quiet. Max had seen Gina and he hadn't mentioned it. Did they meet by arrangement? Was it in passing? Why hadn't he said anything?

'Lovely girl,' Henry added indistinctly.

Everyone seemed to have forgotten I was there. I felt inferior to the wonderful Gina, who his mother was so hell bent on getting him back with. To the Gina who had now been promoted. To the Gina who had 'grown apart' from my boyfriend.

'Oh, I know what we should do.' Clare stopped messing around with her dishes and straightened up. 'How about Gina, Paula and I come to your salon?'

'That would be nice,' I managed. What the …! How the hell would I get through this? How could I possibly welcome Max's ex and her mother with open arms? Clare and Paula, Gina's Mum, were very good friends but I didn't want them doing friendship stuff in my salon. It would be like some form of punishment.

'I think it would,' Clare went on. 'If Gina and Max are friends, it would be nice for you to meet her. Plus, if you two plan on staying together, obviously Paula would be coming to the wedding.'

I was actually not surprised by her assumptions. One minute she thought Max could do better, the next we were getting married. That comment wasn't for my benefit, it was for Max's. She knew I'd be upset that she was imposing his ex-girlfriend into my life, but making such statements about our commitment plans averted Max's suspicion that she didn't like me.

Max didn't bat an eyelid, but drank his wine as if exes and our marriage were things we should be talking about.

I should throw a baby into the circle, really get this conversation started!

Clare served her succulent roast beef. It was perfect, of course. We sat at the solid oak table, the bi-fold doors opened to their full extent, letting in the gentle breeze from the lengthy garden. The pruned lawn and manicured shrubbery were immaculate, the perfect background to the false, happy family we portrayed.

***

When I'd met Clare for the first time, I'd overheard a conversation that to this day I wished I'd not been privy to. I was coming from the kitchen, looking for the bathroom, when I heard her malicious words, 'It's like the *Hillbillies* meets *Pride and Prejudice*. Surely, Max, you can see the difference in your backgrounds? I thought you and Gina were go—'

Max had stopped her. 'Mother, Kat has been through so much, and built a life for herself. She is a lovely woman, who you should admire. The least you could do is show her some respect, for my sake.'

He'd obviously explained my family background. I loved that he'd stood up to his mother for me. I loved that he accepted my unstable upbringing. And from that day forward, Clare never criticised me in front of Max again. No, she used her scheming, underhand ways to integrate her dislike into innocent conversations.

***

Sitting amicably, but burning inside, I tried so hard to consume the mixture of green vegetables, carrots and potatoes all coated with herbs and juices – usually a favourite of mine – but I struggled. I managed about half, then had to excuse myself and apologise that I couldn't possibly eat any more of her 'wonderful cooking'. Yes, I used those words. It was a constant battle to win points, to impress her and make her understand why I was right for Max. It was a relentless battle to show her that 'hillbillies' wasn't how I would describe myself or my family.

Clare, obviously offended at my wasting her good food, was quiet for the rest of the meal. Not a bad thing, I know, but I wanted to get away from her. She had worn me down this afternoon. Feeling less than my normal chirpy self, I now felt beaten into submission. Max noticed my weariness and as he finished his dinner he said we should make a move. I could have hugged him! But Clare looked as if she had been told he'd never come to Sunday dinner again. We waited until Clare and Henry had finished their lunch. I'm sure she slowed down. I could have imagined it, but I think not.

'I'm sorry, Clare.' I actually meant it, as we said our goodbyes. 'I'm not sure what's come over me, I thought this bug was shifting but it's not moving.' The lies came easily. I knew full well this bug wasn't going anywhere unless I did something about it.

'I hope you feel better soon,' Clare said.

In the car on the way home, I told myself to leave it. Don't mention it, it will cause an argument. Leave it!

'So, when did you see Gina?' Okay, I couldn't leave it.

'She was in the pub yesterday.'

'Oh right, so you had a drink with her?'

'No, we passed at the bar and caught up.'

'Caught up, what's that mean?'

'Come on, Kat, you're not serious.' Max looked at me. He smiled as if I was telling him a joke, but I didn't see anything funny. When he realised I wasn't laughing, he shook his head and continued, exasperated. 'I mean that I said, "How are things with you?" She told me about her new job. She told me about her mum, and how her sister had moved away.'

'What did you tell her about you?'

'I told her I'd met this amazing woman who had come into my life and turned my world around.'

'Don't mock me, Max.'

'I'm not mocking you, I just think you're being a little silly.'

'A little silly.' My cool was lost, broken by the tension of the afternoon. 'I've never met this woman who apparently you were so in love with for three years, the woman who seems too busy around in the background whilst I fight your mother to show her I'm the better person.'

'Kat, please, calm—'

'No, Max, this is so unfair.' The tears were coming now, giving me the emotional outlet I felt I deserved. 'I don't talk about my exes as if they were part of my family.'

'My mum is friends with her mum.'

'So that makes it okay, then,' I said sarcastically. 'Why didn't you tell me you'd bumped into her?'

'I didn't think it was important.'

'But you thought it important enough to mention it in front of your mother.'

'Kat, you're losing it here. I have no idea where this has come from. Mum is friends with Paula. You've commented that Mum hasn't been into your salon since she used the vouchers I brought her, and now, not only is she coming, she's bringing two new customers.'

'Oh my God, Max, please take me home before I scream.' Clare had achieved exactly what I thought she'd set out to do, and he'd fallen for it. Was he really that weak?

'Kat, you're becoming a little out of control.' Was he patronising me?

'Out of control!' I screamed. Yes, maybe he was right. It could have been the hormones; to be honest, I have no idea where the rage came from, how it had got to the point where I could have physically harmed him. I let the tears fall as I told him his vindictive mother was not going to make me look like a head-case.

'No, Kat, you're doing that yourself.' The tears pricked as his words stung. He pulled up outside my salon. 'Look, Kat, this has blown out of proportion, let's—'

I slammed the car door. I wasn't sure if I assumed he would chase me. I wasn't sure I wanted him to. He didn't, but I felt his eyes boring into me as I let myself into the side of the building. His car engine roared as the noise of his anger filled the small village.

I couldn't face this.

How could I have his baby when I couldn't bear his mother? What if it had its grandma's personality? I sat against the door, looking up the stairs towards my home, tears escaping, as I thought about what had just happened.

Oh God, what had I done? I should ring him, tell him to come back. But I didn't. I sat, listening, wondering if he would come back. But he didn't. I'd shared a piece of my madness with him, a piece that he could have lived without.

A piece that might persuade him he could live without *me*.

5

Later I called Dad and spoke to Marianne. I decided to eliminate most of the truth, apologising to Marianne for not making it, telling her I'd been feeling really ill. I wasn't lying this time. As always, Marianne understood. She didn't raise her voice, she didn't sound disappointed or elated. She simply told me to take care of myself and get some rest. Her pleasantness annoyed me; why couldn't she be a bit feisty? I felt resentful that she had an air of tranquillity that I'd never found. She talked a lot about Jesus and God. I wondered if the Church had helped her. It annoyed me even more, that she felt she was the one that needed to find peace. She *chose* to move in with our deranged family; but we didn't choose to have her, like we didn't choose for Mum to die.

The softness of my sofa enveloped me, and I lay again, waiting for Max to call. What if he didn't? What would I do about being pregnant then? I knew I should call him, but I couldn't.

I thought back to how his manipulating mother had made sure this argument would happen. I stared at the ceiling remembering how she had described me and my family. She would never have described us as hillbillies if Mum was still around. No. She wouldn't have, because if Mum was still around, we'd have been classed as a 'normal' family.

I know this because we were 'normal' before she died …

***

Being only twelve at the time, I was starting to discover who I was. I'd just started my periods and upped my bra size to a B-cup (okay, so I stuffed it with toilet paper). I'd discovered leg and armpit shaving, although Mum was really upset with me and had said, 'That'll be it now, you'll be at it all the time.' She was even more upset when I shaved my arms; not under them, all over them.

'But I'm so hairy, Mum.' I wasn't. I had a few bum-fluff wisps, but I felt like a gorilla.

I was growing into a woman when Mum died. Hormones were rumbling below the surface, waiting to escape into a firing frenzy. I cried when Dad asked me to pass him the sauce at the dinner table and I shouted when he asked, 'So what have you done at school today?' I accused him of being nosey, of not having trust in me, assuming he was checking that I'd actually gone to school! Sometimes he couldn't handle the random, unprovoked outbursts and he'd shout back or send me to my room. Other times, Mum would give him a nod that meant, 'Leave her.' The word 'HORMONES' explained it all.

I was becoming interested in boys when Mum died. I was having important debates with friends about whether 'French kissing' was actually disgusting, and why do boys feel the need to use tongues? Not that I'd had my first kiss by this time. It was a question still being analysed. Do I kiss Andrew Hopper, or not? If I kiss Andrew Hopper does it mean he's officially my boyfriend? I was going through deep, agonising concerns, worries and torments that took over my every thought. Most of my friends had done the kissing thing and were giving me advice, which entailed practising on mirrors, arms and pillows. This wasn't easy because there was no response from these material objects.

I was a teenager in the making. A teenager with attitude, a teenager with a family to stretch to their limits and try out some arbitrary outburst on, whilst trying to understand what the hell was going on with my body!

Then it was over. Then she wasn't there. No warning. No nothing. She was gone.

A reckless young lad driving too fast had lost control. Instantly, they said. Instant. 'She didn't feel a thing,' they said. I didn't argue,

'How do you know?' even though these thoughts were at the forefront of my mind. 'How do you know how she felt?' I wanted to scream at them. The young lad was okay, though; broke both his legs but they healed and he walked again.

He saw his family again.

Dad was a complete mess. Mum's sister, Aunty June, practically moved in. Libby didn't really understand. She kept asking questions, but I didn't talk about it. I didn't know what to say. I was the older one, but I was only twelve. I remember sitting in my bedroom alone for hours.

'Are you okay?' Aunty June would ask.

'I'm fine,' I would lie. I just wanted to be alone.

Dad couldn't handle her death. He couldn't cope. About a month after Mum died, coming home from school had become an effort in itself. I had to call at the primary school to pick up Libby. Once we were home I would cook the tea, do the dishes, bath Libby and put her to bed. Dad became an object in the house, an ornament waiting to be dusted and settled back down again. He simply didn't function. It was as if he'd lost his soul and his reason for being.

My contribution just happened. Dad didn't force me to do it. It felt like the right thing to do. Well, the only thing to do, really. I soon forgot about kissing boys and even let my leg hair grow. Nothing really mattered. The feeling of being trapped and alone was dreadful.

The afternoon when everything came to ahead he was lying on the sofa, shaking and crying, his red, sore eyes looking pitifully at me. Covered in a pink fleece blanket (Libby's bedtime comfort) he looked lost and lonely; timid and terrified. He cried more tears when I asked, 'Aren't you well, Dad?' I ushered Libby into the kitchen, opened a full packet of chocolate biscuits which I'd bought secretly and stashed away for moments when I wanted to bribe her. After ringing Aunty June – as all I could get from Dad was, 'I can't live', 'I don't want to.' – I'm not really sure what happened after that. I just remember nurses coming in an ambulance and taking him away. Aunty June called it 'respite'. She packed our belongings and we went to stay with her.

Libby told everyone at school that her daddy had a 'bite and couldn't live with us anymore'. I was hauled in by the head teacher as they had tried and failed to contact my father; they were concerned. I thought they were being downright nosey. I told them he wasn't well and we were spending some time with our aunty. It escalated; they wanted her number. They wanted to chat with her, so she told me. Check I wasn't lying, more like.

I think Mum would have been proud of her sister. She was married to my Uncle Ernest. A quiet, unassuming man, who didn't say much. He watched the television, read the newspaper and sometimes did the garden. They didn't have children but it was never discussed; well, not in my presence anyway.

When Dad came out of hospital, Marianne came with him. Marianne was a nurse. I assumed that's how she and Dad met; I didn't ask. Once she arrived on the scene, it was hard. Life was hard before but having this woman there every minute was unbearable. It was within weeks after Marianne arrived that Aunty June moved away. I hated Marianne for that too. It was obvious it was her fault that Aunty June suddenly disappeared. I'd begged Dad to let us go with her, but he wasn't listening. I'd thought about running away but I'd have had to take Libby with me. I was worried something would happen to her, or something would happen to me and she'd be left alone. So, we were trapped. I soon lost any interest in finding Aunty June when the contact seemed to cease. I thought that Marianne was hiding letters from her, so I was first to pick up the letters from the dirty mat, where the clean envelopes would gather. But nothing. After about six months I gave up.

I'd gathered as I'd become an adult that the mechanics of our family were not like a smooth-running car travelling along flawless roads. No, we'd decided to take a different journey, the bumpy one, filled with discomfort, disappointment and often pain.

I didn't like Marianne; I merely tolerated her. She had her feet well and truly tucked under the table from the day she walked into our home. Dad was still a mess, suffering with severe depression, and had started to drink. He lost his job as a site manager because of constant absences, being late or drunk.

Marianne stepped straight into Mum's role. She never mentioned Mum to me and Libby, which pleased me because I didn't want to speak to her about Mum, but at the same time it enraged me because it was as if Mum had never existed. I hated Dad at the time. I'd have outbursts and call Marianne names, which I won't repeat. But let me explain, before you think I was some kind of spoilt brat. This woman came into our lives and took over from another woman who, in my eyes, was amazing; she was my mum. I remember one time being so vicious to Marianne that I made her cry. Dad came into the kitchen, although he had no idea what had happened, but because she was crying he slapped me. He had never hit me before.

'I hate you!' I'd told him. I'd said it steadily, evenly and quietly. The worst thing is, I actually meant it. I pushed past him, needing to be alone in my bedroom. I gathered that would be the place they would send me anyway.

It took a few days before Dad spoke to me. Not that I was bothered. I felt so much hatred towards him. He told me I needed to apologise to Marianne. I did and she'd sat me down and I expected a big stepmother lecture, or her turning me into a frog, or something just as bizarre, if I ever pulled a trick like that again. But she didn't. She cried. She cried when she told me how much she loved Dad (Dad, who spent most of his life drunk, asleep or crying). She said she thought she was his angel who'd been brought down to support him (that's when it occurred to me she also had issues). She cried even more when she told me how in awe of Mum she was and how she didn't want to replace her. I told her that was good, because under no circumstances would that happen. She could never replace my mum and I would never love her the way I'd loved my mum. I wasn't sure I could ever love her (although I didn't tell her that).

We grew as a dysfunctional family. Over the months and years our father's depression became worse. He turned even more to alcohol to try and dispel his emotions but it didn't work. I became Libby's surrogate mother, or that's what it felt like. I always worried about her, felt responsible for her and wanted to protect her. The feeling of completely safeguarding her never, ever, went away. I didn't, and never have, liked that feeling; a constant ache, wanting to ensure all is okay. Why anyone would choose to have that responsibility is beyond me.

I often wondered what Mum would have thought. I wondered if she would think I was selfish for having doubts about having the baby. I always imagined Mum to be maternal, but actually I'm not sure if she was; there was no-one to ask. She was great with us; we were good friends. We'd have a film, takeaway and popcorn on Friday nights. She would pick us up from school, we'd head straight to the local video hire shop and we'd all pick a film each. She would pick some other film which she would watch with Dad when we'd gone to bed. I would beg to stay up and watch it with them and she'd say, 'When you're a bit older.'

That never happened.

So, although she was fun to be around, I often wondered if she was naturally maternal. Some women do have to work at it (apparently so; I've heard customers say this is the case). It's conversations like this I would've loved to have had with Mum. I often wondered, if she was around would I be more inclined to have my own family? If she'd been there I wouldn't have lived with a burning incompleteness that ate away at me.

***

Lying on the sofa I closed my eyes, trying to connect with her like I often did, taking in the smells of the burning candles, engrossing myself in my need for her.

'Come on, Mum, what shall I do?' I asked aloud. 'What would you do?' I found it comforting and cathartic to try and feel some kind of connection with her. I often asked her questions and I wondered if she showed me the answers in different ways. But let's make it clear here: if she had shown herself I would probably have passed out.

I stared at my mobile, wondering if Max had gone home, gone to Joe's or Lawrence's, gone back to his Mum's or even gone to Gina's. I knew the latter wouldn't be true but now these unruly thoughts were swimming around in my mind, it was hard not to exaggerate. What if he discussed my behaviour with Joe and Lawrence? I liked them and they seemed to like me; but if they thought I was an irrational girlfriend, would they be telling Max to get out? 'I'd leave, mate, it can only get worse.' I could hear their virile tones in my mind as I wondered what would be the best thing to do to solve this.

I couldn't bring myself to ring him. I wasn't sure how to explain myself without telling him the truth, or if using my hormones as an excuse was immoral. It was simply best to stay away.

He would call me when he was ready.

Hopefully.

6

The banging sensation rattled through my body, shaking me into reality. Someone was making their presence known at the front door. Max? 8.30a.m! Jesus, how did that happen? I quickly pulled myself off the sofa where I'd fallen asleep, a little embarrassed that I'd not changed into my nightwear and whoever was at the door would be able to tell. I took off my jeans and put on my dressing gown; vain, I know. I felt unstable enough with these hormonal outbursts without my unkempt tattiness being added to the equation.

The banging became louder; someone was desperate to be in. Had Max come to talk things through? I unlatched the door and found a red-faced, sweaty Melanie.

'Where have you been? Have you just got up?' Melanie looked perturbed by my dishevelled appearance. Probably worried I was going to leave her alone in the salon again; she'd practically begged me not to after the Mrs D incident. But her reason for letting Sophie treat Mrs D was so weak that I didn't feel I *could* leave her in the salon alone. Not that she wasn't capable, I knew she was, but telling me she didn't like Mrs D and she thought Sophie was more than efficient at waxing had really annoyed me. She and I had agreed something and she'd gone back on her word. But I'd let it go. I had bigger things on my mind; I couldn't deal with staff issues, plus, Melanie was too lovely to fall out with.

I'd totally forgotten she was coming for a shower. Suzy trained her three times a week before work. It seemed pointless her going back home to get ready to come to work, so with my flat being above the salon it made sense she came here to get ready. I would make us breakfast; just coffee and toast but it made Melanie's life a little easier.

She was getting married in four weeks and to be quite honest, she'd put me and most of our customers off ever wanting to get married. Her wedding was stressing her out, what with her interfering mother and scatty sister. Nothing seemed to have gone to plan, from suppliers going bust to bridesmaids falling pregnant; trust me – that was just the tip of the iceberg. So, I liked helping her, if only in a small way, as I didn't think she was getting much support of late.

After following me upstairs she showered quickly and appeared looking sophisticated in her bright-pink tunic, her fine blonde hair tied back, her make-up naturally applied, giving her a flawless complexion that many of our customers envied. She'd been training with Suzy for three months and the difference in her posture and silhouette was amazing, not to mention her confidence. I'd never thought of her as someone who needed to lose weight but fourteen pounds later her trim figure had me envying her dedication to achieve it. Suzy would rattle on at me about training with them. Not that she thought I needed to lose weight but my whinging about the extra pounds got no sympathy from Suzy. My laid-back or couldn't-be-bothered approach would have her urging, 'Seriously, your best friend's a bloody personal trainer. We could be walking around the park instead of sitting and drinking wine.' I would weigh it up, seriously think about it. 'Wine or a run?' A big decision to make; but the wine always won.

'So, how are you feeling?'

'Tired.' I couldn't lie about that fact; the darkness around my eyes and my pasty skin was letting everyone know I was absolutely knackered.

'It's a hell of a virus, you really should go to the doctor's,' Melanie said, sipping the coffee I'd made her.

'I will,' I nodded. 'Look, I'll jump in the shower, then I'll be down.' I couldn't have this conversation with her, not because I did trust her but the more people who knew the truth, the more the word could spread. If I decided that having a baby wasn't the right thing for me, I didn't want to be judged. I didn't want people to think badly of me.

In the shower, I placed my hand over my stomach, which was actually protruding (well, more than usual). Maybe it was my imagination or maybe it was the dinner from yesterday. Maybe I thought it was bigger than it was. Some people have had babies and didn't even know they were pregnant, so why would I be showing? I wanted to research it, I wanted to understand what was happening to my body. But I knew if I did that I'd become attached, I'd find out that what I thought of as an egg would become a growing baby. I wasn't sure how far on I was but imagined eight or nine weeks. I was worried I'd find out it had arms, legs, a full head of hair and was citing the alphabet. For now, ignorance was safe. I'd not allowed myself to emotionally connect or believe that I could be a mum.

Dressed in a black tunic I looked every bit the professional therapist I aspired to be. I had the same pink tunic as Melanie but the black hid the couple of pounds I'd gained recently. My make-up masked my grey, tired skin and my trained fingers artistically enhanced my dull eyes. Melanie wasn't in the flat, so I knew she'd have gone downstairs to open the salon. Usually we had fifteen minutes spare but not this morning.

I wished Libby was more like Melanie. Melanie was two years older than Libby but Melanie had worked for me since she was Libby's age. She seemed more mature and established. I'm not putting Libby down, as I loved my sister's quirky ways, but sometimes I wished she'd take life a little more seriously. On the other hand, I thought Melanie too young to be getting married, but I wouldn't tell her that. Maybe Libby could meet me somewhere in the middle; maybe a passion or dream to follow, instead of wondering how much she could drink over the weekend. Desperate for her to enjoy her new job, I thought it best to see if she was out of bed.

'I'm just leaving the house now,' she answered, obviously annoyed by my interference.

'Won't you be late?'

'Hopefully, then they might sack me.'

'Libby, for God's sake, come on, look for another job.'

'Yeah, yeah, will do, got to go or I *will* be late, 'bye.' She was gone.

Sometimes I wished I could just be her sister instead of a mother figure. I wondered what Mum would have done in this situation. Would she have let her go and do her own thing, make her own mistakes? I didn't know. I couldn't ask anyone. Aunty June was no longer around. Marianne wouldn't know because she didn't know Mum. I couldn't ask Dad because every time I mentioned Mum's name his eyes would glaze over, sometimes even watering. I wondered how Marianne could live with a man who loved another woman. More than loved: he'd never got over her. He suffered Mum's loss daily, but he'd chosen to have Marianne in our lives. Why had she put herself through that? But once again, it wasn't something I wanted to ask her. Not because I didn't want to know but because a connection to Marianne was like a betrayal of Mum. I couldn't let Marianne into my heart, into my world, as it was Mum's place and she wasn't replaceable. Acceptance was probably the best way to describe my feelings towards Marianne; I accepted that she was there.

The warmth of the sunshine shimmered through the windows as I walked into the salon. *Temple Spa Quietude* hit me as soon as I opened the door. It was our daily routine to spray the relaxing mist, bringing tranquillity into our space. I was pleased it wasn't a smell that I'd become turned off by, like many other delicate sprays. The whiteness of the walls reflected the purity of the ambience I wanted to create. The only decoration was in the form of a windswept woman's face, a painted portrait by a local artist. It took up the back wall. It was a dramatic piece, which gave vogue and elegance to the calm setting. The black outline defined her high cheekbones, her closed eyes and her sensual features. Her lips were bright red. The flower in her hair matched the lustre of the deep colour.

Melanie was talking on the phone, signalling for me to come over. The wooden floor echoed my footsteps and I wished it didn't when I realised Melanie was mouthing 'Clare' to me. I waved my hands at her, mouthing 'no', as Melanie shrugged her shoulders, looked flustered and said, 'Yes she's here.' I rolled my eyes and shook my head. She mimed 'sorry' as if she couldn't have done anything else.

'Morning, Clare, this is early.' I smiled although she couldn't see me: I knew through many training courses that this helped to project a positive sounding tone.

'Early?' She laughed. 'We're halfway through the day! Anyway, I spoke with Paula last night. Gina's off work today and they would love to come into the salon for manicures.'

'Clare, it's Monday, I'm fully booked.' I wished I could put the words back in, although it was true, names were crammed into our diary, Clare would think I was being obstructive. But there'd be no time to pee, let alone face the rudeness of Clare, Max's ex and her mother!

'Oh.' Her indignation apparent. 'Well, I did try to call you last night but there was no answer.'

She had, but I'd ignored her call. Not that it would have made any difference: the diary was full anyway. 'Can you hold for a second?'

'If I must.'

I didn't answer her curt remark, as I placed her on hold. I could see my mobile flashing Max's name. I was dying to answer his call, hear his voice, ask how he was, apologise for my troubled behaviour, but I couldn't leave Clare on hold any longer than necessary. I felt hostility rising again, that Clare was forcing Gina into my life. I wanted to tell Clare that we couldn't possibly do any treatments for them – but I was actually curious about Gina. What did she look like? Was she like me or were we completely different? What interests did she have? As these thoughts collided, I met Melanie's gaze. 'Please can you work late tonight?'

'Bit short notice.'

'I know, but its Clare and she wants to bring Max's ex and her mum.'

'No! That's awful. I won't work late if she's doing that to you.'

'I'll pay you double.'

'Okay, if you insist.' She was quick to answer and I knew paying her double wasn't actually worth them coming in for treatments; but I wanted to keep Clare happy. Or was it that I wanted to meet Gina? I wasn't sure, but whichever, I needed Melanie's help.

'Oh God, this is going to be torture.' Melanie said. I picked up the phone again, quickly agreed to Clare's request, then double-checked she'd definitely hung up before we embarked on a great discussion about her inability to be polite.

***

Clare's first encounter with us was through a voucher which Max had bought her. I thought back to how I'd been drawn to Max from the first time I'd met him. His smile had seemed nervous but genuine. One hand clutched his wallet as he ran the other through his thick blond waves (not long hair, might I add). His deep-blue eyes were warm and genuine as I'd asked if I could help him. 'Christmas present?' I'd asked. We were used to men coming to the salon in the deep, dark months of December, with instructions from their wives.

'Yes, hopefully,' he'd grinned. 'A friend's girlfriend recommended you.'

'Great.' Was he single?

'I'd like a voucher for my mother.' Singlehood was looking likely!

'Okay, were you looking to get her a particular treatment?'

'I don't know what she'd like, or what you do.' He laughed, seemingly embarrassed about his ignorance.

I found it endearing. 'Okay.' I'd laughed with him, trying to make him feel comfortable in what was obviously an alien environment. 'Well, I could go through the treatments with you.' Mrs D was being treated at the time and interrupted with a cough. 'Or you can give her an open voucher that lets her choose her own treatments.'

'That's a better idea.' He relaxed, obviously relieved that he wasn't going to be talked through a catalogue of waxing, massaging and tanning.

'Right, well, our average treatment is about £20, so if we were to look at, for example—'

'If I spent £100, would this give her a few treatments?'

'Yes, about four or five treatments, depending which one she chose. But surely she doesn't need that much?'

'Oh, she does.'

'I'm sure she's not that bad.' I'd laughed.

He'd grinned, probably realising that what he'd said was an insult to his mother. I picked out my professional vouchers, proudly displaying them to him. They were pink and elegant; gold writing swirled across the card, perfectly symbolising the stylish image I wanted the salon to project. I could see he was impressed as I penned '£100' on the gift card then placed it into a pale pink envelope which included a real feather.

'Great,' he said, nodding his obvious appreciation for our personal touch. He looked around, his gaze stopping at my windswept lady. 'That's stunning! Who did that?'

'A local artist,' I told him. His excitement was hard to miss, as he went on to tell me that he was working on a few projects at the moment and this type of design would be great. I gave him the artist's contact number.

'See – it's fate. You were meant to come in here!'

'Fate.' He smiled, and as our eyes connected a tingle of excitement raced through my body. It sounds corny, I know, and it was only for a second, but it was there. Something had happened, something exciting.

Then he left.

A few weeks later, his mother visited the salon, with the vouchers; she used them all in one day. We'd treated her to a manicure, pedicure, a facial and a massage. She was hell, obnoxious as soon as she'd walked through the door. Even Melanie took an instant dislike to her – and Melanie likes everyone (except Mrs D). She'd looked around the salon like she'd come to the dog groomers. Her nostrils had flared as she commented on the candle smells; she wasn't 'attuned' to them. She'd said it was kind of Maxwell (which is how I found out Max's name) to buy her the vouchers but he should have known she didn't visit backstreet salons. Rockcliffe Hall and Seaham Hall were her usual haunts. She'd laughed and said, 'Men! Sometimes they don't think.' To be honest, after her nightmare visit, Max had kind of faded from my fantasies.

If only I'd kept thinking that way.

For the first time ever, I wished I'd never seen him again. I wished he'd never entered my life. We'd had an amazing six months but I was now in a situation I'd never wanted to be in. I didn't want children.

I loved the idea of the cornflake box family, the perfect ideal, but I didn't think I truly believed in it. I'd grown up fast when Mum died, mainly because I had Libby to look after. I didn't want her looking at me as a failure and I didn't want her to be a failure.

I wasn't ready and I didn't know if I would ever be ready to have a baby. A child I was totally responsible for; a child who depended on me. I wasn't sure I could go through it again. I hadn't enjoyed the pressure of the responsibility I'd had for Libby, and still had. I was scared. I was scared of loving something so dearly and it being taken away from me.

Like Mum was.

I'd heard so many disturbing stories from customers, how children had been ripped away from their parents by tragic accidents or fatal diseases. 'To lose a child is the worst thing. The parent is supposed to go before the child.' I hadn't heard this statement just once. It had been said numerous times. So many, I'd lost count.

I didn't know what it was like to lose a child; but I did know what it was like to lose a parent. If losing a child was worse, then why would I purposely bring a child into this world? Why would I want to live with the fear? I would be terrified that I could lose something so precious, so easily. I still hurt so much about Mum. Why would I bring something into my life that one day might cause me more pain?

I could hear Suzy's voice: 'You can't live your life like that.' But I could. I had to. I had to protect all the emotional dignity I had left. I had to feel safe and having a child wouldn't allow me that. I wasn't sure I could live my life in fear.

That's why I was ignoring Max's calls. That's why I didn't want to hear his voice. I needed to make a decision.

It would be easier if he wasn't in my life.

I wished I'd never met him.

7

The day was slow in comparison to others. Although we were both really busy, the arrival of Clare, Gina and Paula was hanging over me. I felt tired and the sickness hadn't eased much. I tried to eat oat biscuits, as apparently, they can help with morning sickness, but I had all-day and all-night sickness. However, I had to override the nausea and serve my customers. If I decided not to bring this baby into the world, I could stop this queasiness immediately. What was stopping me from booking an appointment and ending this nightmare? Max? If I ended the pregnancy, he wouldn't need to know a thing. But could I live with myself if I did that?

It was Clare who walked in first, her boldness filling the salon. Gina and Paula followed humbly behind her. They looked uncomfortable as they smiled at me, staying in Clare's shadow.

'Hello, Kathryn, wonderful that you could fit us in. I told them you wouldn't be busy.'

'Busy? We've opened late—'

I interrupted Melanie hastily. 'It's lovely to see you all.'

Melanie turned away, probably swearing to herself. I felt her frustration but had to leave it. I wanted to make a good impression with Clare, and with Max's ex. I didn't want to mess up so that they could discuss me later; all agreeing that Gina was better for Max than I was.

Clare and Paula sat at the nail stations whilst Gina said she would wait.

I wanted to study Gina. I wanted to establish the colour of her eyes, her features and the softness of her skin.

I wanted to see what it was that Max had once loved about her.

'So, we've been out for lunch today and shopped all around York, haven't we, girls?' Clare said. 'This finishes the day off perfectly.'

'Did you buy anything nice?' I asked. I wasn't really interested; well, maybe a little interested in Gina's purchases. Her choices might give me some understanding of her personality. So, as Clare reeled off a list of dresses, shoes and accessories (brand names included) I waited for Gina to speak. But she sat quietly, watching us intently. Her silence was unnerving. I didn't like her ability to make me so tense in my own environment.

Melanie was happy to chat about her wedding, telling them all the problems she'd had. I was tired of hearing about the wedding. There were only so many times I could hear about the photographer going bust and how her wedding dress had only just arrived. However, today I was grateful for her stories because they eased the tension.

Paula was lovely. I wondered how come she was friends with Clare. I couldn't imagine Paula being as offensive as Clare often was. Although Clare had toned it down somewhat whilst she was in my salon, she still had an air of self-importance about her as she sat watching me. I finished Clare and got ready to engage with Gina and find out more about her. She smiled warmly at me as she sat in Clare's seat. I responded kindly, telling her to make herself comfortable.

She had short dark hair, curls that surrounded her petite face and chocolate-coloured eyes that were warm and inviting. She was smaller than me, only by an inch or so, but she looked fragile compared to my robust figure. Her thin waist and tiny frame were so much more delicate than I'd imagined. Max was tall and broad. If she hadn't have been so pretty I would have thought she'd pale into insignificance next to him. They must have been a stunning couple. I felt a lump rise in my throat. My thoughts moved quickly to them having babies, how beautiful their children would be. I blinked back a tear and rubbed my nose.

'Are you okay?' Gina asked, her voice soft and genuine.

'I'm fine,' I lied. 'It's just a cold, or something.'

'Kat hasn't been well all week. She needs to go to the doctor's,' Melanie announced.

'There's so much going around at the moment,' Gina said.

I hated that she seemed so nice. I wanted her to be horrible. It would have made me understand why she and Max had split up. I hated that they had simply grown apart; I hated that one of them had not done something so unforgiveable that they would never get back together. I know many couples grow apart permanently, but I felt unsettled that Max and Gina still liked each other.

'Wasn't Joe feeling poorly?' Paula said.

Gina blushed a little. 'Yes, he was a little under the weather,' she managed, not meeting my eye. I watched as she stared at her mother, who seemed oblivious to the awkward undercurrents.

'Joe who?' Clare asked. 'Maxwell's friend Joe?'

'Yes,' Paula said, still seemingly unaware of her daughter's discomfort. 'Gina's been seeing him for a few weeks now, haven't you, pet?'

'Yes, Mum.' I couldn't work out whether she was gritting her teeth. She looked at me, rolling her eyes. 'It's only been a few weeks, so we're seeing how it goes before announcing it to the whole world.'

'I didn't know you were seeing Joe.' Clare's lips tightened as she spoke.

'I haven't told anyone. We were, as I said, seeing how it would go.'

'So, is it going well?' Clare was still brusque. I was actually thankful for once that Clare was so outspoken, as I too wanted to know these details. I also felt comforted that it wasn't only me she was abrupt with.

'At the moment, yes, it is.' Gina smiled. She looked happy but still uncomfortable talking about her new relationship.

Melanie quickly changed the subject; she was so good at sensing any tension. She went into a rendition of how she and

Bobby had met. I'd heard this story endlessly but appreciated her chatty and personable nature as the ladies listened with obvious interest. Gina seemed grateful also, as she laughed along with the others.

The treatments seemed to take longer than usual and the relief was overwhelming when they were finally over. I felt my shoulders unwind, the tension release as they left my salon, comparing nails, smiling and laughing. But then Gina turned around, mouthing something to Clare and Paula and pointing in my direction. My stomach twisted.

'She's coming back,' Melanie mumbled.

'I know,' I said, between gritted teeth.

'Hi again.'

'Hi, is everything okay?' I smiled.

'Yes.' She came to face me, opposite the reception desk. 'Look, I wanted to apologise for us coming here today.'

'I don't mind.' More lies.

'I know how forceful Clare can be. Deep down she really does have a heart of gold, once you break through that hard shell. I really thought it was unfair us coming here, but she insisted you'd insisted.'

'Well, I did say it was good idea.' I smiled.

'You probably didn't have a choice.' She laughed, her eyes soft as she spoke gently. 'I just wanted to say sorry for coming, but it was lovely to meet you, and Max is very lucky.'

'Thank you.' I was surprised and felt the need to return her friendliness. Was there something underlying or was she really this nice? 'Joe is very lucky too.'

She thanked me again before leaving.

I watched her walk away. I started to understand what Clare liked about Gina. I also understood the connection between these ladies: Clare felt included in Gina's life. I thought about how she hadn't been included in mine. I'd not offered her a friendship in the way Gina had. Could I have done? Clare and Paula, close friends, with their children dating; it was so cosy. I came from a completely different background. Not that I wasn't willing to try for a friendship with Clare but I didn't want a mother figure. I'd survived this long without any mothering aspect to my life. Marianne had never been someone I would have called a mother. I didn't even refer to her as my step mum; she was Dad's girlfriend.

'She was lovely.' Melanie interrupted my thoughts, as I analysed my own mixed-up life.

'I know, isn't it awful?' I cried out to Melanie, who smiled at my dramatics.

'You don't need to worry about her. Look at you!'

'I'm a bloody mess at the moment,' I said.

Suddenly my phone rang. Max? No, Suzy. The photo of her sticking out her tongue flashed impatiently at me.

'Oh God, Kat, it's awful,' she said, the minute I answered.

'What is?' My own worries vanished immediately.

'He's married.'

8

After establishing that Suzy was talking about Michael, her new boyfriend, I told her to come straight over.

Before she arrived, I called Libby. I didn't want her to think I was stalking her but I was so concerned that she would lose her job. I wanted her to acquire a sense of responsibility and take a grasp of her life.

'It was crap.' Her words were slurred. I knew she'd probably already drunk a bottle of wine.

I could hear chattering and laughter in the background. 'It's a Monday night, Libby.'

'And …?'

'You're not having a party, are you?' I know I sounded prudish but I didn't do the whole student thing. I thought Libby should be trying to grow out of that. Dad's drinking also flashed a warning at the back of my mind. Don't get me wrong, I like a drink. Well, not at the moment, but usually I was partial to a glass of wine or two. But I thought Libby's drinking was getting out of control. 'You've got work in the morning.'

'For fuck's sake, Kat, I've only had a few. Will you stop going on.'

Her harsh words threw me. She'd never sworn at me before. She'd always shown me respect in her own way, appreciating all I'd done for her as we were growing up. 'Right, I'll call you tomorrow,' I told her sternly, my mothering tendencies to the forefront.

Hanging up the phone, I touched my stomach. Most pregnant women would find this exciting; but I didn't. I felt sick at the thought of bringing a child into this world and having to be accountable for its actions.

I felt it was my fault that Libby was behaving like this. She had so much potential, so much to give. She could be teaching kids in the field of sciences, leading the way, fulfilling her life in so many ways.

I wanted her to make Mum proud, in the way I'd felt I made her proud when I opened my salon. Mum's advice was that every woman should have a therapist. She'd meant a beauty therapist. Mum was by no means a prima donna who believed we're only here to look good and serve our man. No: therapy was, for her, a relaxation technique which she believed every woman should benefit from. By having her therapy, she looked good and felt better. She always had a weekly appointment with her 'therapist'. Eyebrows shaped, nails manicured and massage savoured. It kept her sane. I was only starting to find these things out when she passed away. I was starting to be interested in make-up; she was trying to discourage the foundation and encourage the cleansing. 'If you've got to wear that stuff, you must clean it off before you go to bed,' she would say. 'And you're not wearing it for school.'

So, it felt like my destiny to help other women. In opening my own salon I'd achieved my dream and Mum would have been bursting with pride. I wished I could tell her I understood it now: my salon wasn't only about helping women look good, it *was* therapy. It was a place where women could express their feelings and tell us their worries. They came to us because we didn't judge them. We understood. As women, we let out our worries, concerns and even tears, but we also relish laughter and joy as we share wonderful life stories. I'd created a sanctuary for women that enabled them to release emotion, talk freely and walk out feeling liberated, refreshed and pretty damn good.

I wished I could get Libby to understand how having a purpose in life could help her feel closer to Mum. Libby's only purpose was to have fun; but I'm not sure her life *was* fun. I also knew, though, that I had to stop judging her.

Max was ringing when Suzy arrived. I had to ignore the call because Suzy was sobbing uncontrollably. Great big huge, loud, heartfelt sobs. Her breath was coming in gasps, her shoulders shaking to the rhythm of her pain, as she desperately struggled to tell her story. All I could hear was 'wife' and 'big boobs'. Tears rolled down her cheeks, her face was red and screwed up. She looked a complete mess.

After I'd poured her a glass of wine she finally calmed down but resembled someone who'd been in a fight. Her face was puffy, her mascara had spread across her cheeks, leaving a black, smudgy mask.

'Right, tell me again, but slowly.'

'They were coming out of Saltino's,' Suzy said. 'I stopped him. He just looked at me. How could I have been so frigging stupid, Kat?'

'You're not stupid.' I leaned into hug her.

'It's obvious. All the times he's cancelled, the fact we don't go out much.'

'Max and I went out with you both. We would never have guessed he was married.'

It was true. We'd only met him once but I'd put that down to him being an investment banker, always away on business, wanting to spend his free time alone with Suzy.

'She was perfect. What was he doing with me?' Her sobs began again, as she rested her head on my shoulder.

I rubbed her arm, trying to comfort her, take away her pain. 'Look, you are stunning, don't be—'

'Seriously, Kat, I think she'd had a boob job; they were massive, and so pert.' She let out another cry. 'I don't have boobs!'

'Come on.' I held her close. 'I bet she's a bitch, really. I mean, why else would he go looking elsewhere?' It was the only thing I could say to make her feel better but she sobbed into her wine glass, shaking her head, absolutely devastated.

'He told her I was his fitness coach from the gym.' More sobs erupted as she blew her nose into a tissue.

'Look, sweetie, he's a tosser and I'm sorry he's done this to you.'

'I love him,' she cried. 'I know it's only been a few weeks, but this was different. He was so lovely to be around, he made me laugh, we had the same sense of humour, he bought me gifts every time he visited.' More sobs into another tissue as I continued to rub her back. 'I thought he loved me too.'

'Oh, Suz, I wish I could do something.'

I felt hopeless. Suzy always bounced through life, taking everything in her stride. Nothing was ever a problem. She found a solution to everything. Whenever *I* lost *my* cool she would bring me back down to earth. And now she needed me.

***

Suzy had been my rock when Mum died. I loved her for it. I loved that as the years progressed she was always the one I could turn to. Her own mother always offered so much love and friendship, and she had extended that hand to me. I'd taken it and become part of their family. Libby and I were often invited over for dinner. It was such a warm, loving family.

Until Suzy's father cheated.

He left one day, because he couldn't play happy families anymore. He'd found himself a younger version to play with.

Suzy's mother was devastated. She wasn't drinking, like Dad, but her depression was dreadful. At least with Dad, I could ignore him, but ignoring Suzy's mum felt rude. Suzy braved her way through it all. I once said to her, 'You can cry to me.' She'd hugged me close and said, 'I have nothing to cry about. I still have both my parents.'

She'd been the childhood friend that everyone should have. We'd skipped through our primary years together, muddled through our hormonal teenage years together, discovered night-clubbing, getting drunk and hangovers together. She'd seen the worst of me, the best of me and all the parts in between. When Mum died, Suzy protected me; she didn't let anyone hurt me. School was hard; some of the girls I'd believed were close friends distanced themselves. When looking back, I saw that it was me that became distant; isolating myself away from them all. They were too young to know how to handle me, how to approach me. Some of them were quite insensitive and actually wanted to know how it happened.

Suzy shielded me from all of this. She saw the effects Mum's death had on all of us. She saw Dad, the jovial, fun man who used to joke with us, asking questions like, 'Does Suzy have a boyfriend?' (Knowing we'd turn scarlet and deny all knowledge that boys existed) turn into a pitiful, miserable, angry man who couldn't bear people around him. She understood because her mother's outlook was the same for a while, though she eventually pulled herself together and remarried five years later. Luckily Suzy loved her stepfather and he thought the world of her. So, she had two happy families. I was never jealous of her, although I wished I had that loving security; but I also felt extremely lucky to have her as my best friend.

***

As she lay sleeping on my sofa, I wondered if I should call Michael and tell him how stupid he'd been. How he'd probably just lost the best thing that had happened to him. But I knew Suzy would kill me, her dignity and pride extremely important to her. She wouldn't want him to know how horrendous she was feeling. She would pull herself together and move on.

That's what I needed to do: pull myself together.

I needed to speak to Max.

9

'Hi.' I spoke softly, not wanting to wake Suzy. I hadn't expected him to answer at such a late hour. I took the phone into my bedroom, shutting the door quietly. The bedside light cast a soothing glow across the purple and silver covers. I sat cross-legged on the bottom of the bed, feeling the smoothness of the quilt with my fingers.

'Kat, look, I'm sorry I upset you.' Max seemed so relieved to hear my voice, I felt a stab of guilt as I thought how difficult and hysterical I'd been.

'I'm sorry I was such a bitch.'

'You weren't, I get it. I didn't think I'd ever get to talk to you after today.'

'I'm fine.' I smiled. The fact that he 'got it' made me feel so much better. Not having to explain that I was some kind of deranged lunatic. 'I just have to ask, though, but I'm not sure I want to know the answer.'

'Don't ask, then,' he said, which reminded me of something Suzy would say.

'I have to ask,' I said, 'because I need to know.' If I didn't ask it would eat me up. It would work its way through me every day. He was quiet, but I could hear his quiet breathing and wished he was close to me. 'Why did you split up?'

'I've told you. We grew apart.'

'I know, but she's so lovely. She's beautiful—'

'So are you.'

'No, but she's so perfect, she's tiny, she's gorgeous, she's a nice person.'

'She's not perfect to me. You're perfect to me.'

'Did you practise that one?' I jested.

'Look, Gina and I are nothing but friends. I can't even say we're friends because we don't see each other. Seriously, it had ended long before we faced up to it. Kat, it's you I love.'

'I love you too.' I smiled, a lump forming in my throat at how close I had come to walking away from something so special. My inability to face anymore hurt in my life meant that I made irrational choices that injured not only me, but other people too.

'Can I see you?' he asked, as if he were asking me out on a first date. I found myself giggling, small flutters bouncing inside my stomach as I told him, 'Of course.' He said he would pick me up at seven the next evening.

It would be the perfect time to tell him. I couldn't leave it any longer. It wasn't fair on him, me or our baby.

Once I'd covered Suzy with a blanket, I climbed into my own bed.

My mind was swimming. I replayed Max's words as I lay in the dark. I thought back to the next meeting I'd had with him after he'd bought his mum's vouchers …

***

I was singing away, a not-so-tuneful version of *If This Ain't Love* as I wiggled my bum to the rhythm, pretending I was Sophie Ellis-Bextor. I was her, I was on the stage and the crowds were shouting … you get the picture. The door chimed as he walked in. I was shaking my backside as my 36Ds bounced up and down and I jiggled around as if I were having a seizure.

'Great song. I love that one,' he'd laughed.

My face had burned, as my mouth dried up and my whole body blazed with embarrassment.

'Oh, hi. We're not open yet.'

What???? Why did I say that?? I didn't want him to leave!

'Oh sorry, what time do you open? I'll come back.' He looked deflated and as for me, if my cheeks didn't calm down, the heat rushing through my head would make me explode.

'Oh, don't be silly, how can I help?' I spoke to him like a child as I waved my hand in his direction. What was I doing? One minute I was telling him he couldn't be here, the next I was calling him silly for thinking such thoughts.

'I was on my way to work and I was thinking I should get some more vouchers.'

'For who?' I'd asked brazenly. 'Sorry, not that it matters to me who they're for.' I'd laughed, a fake, high-pitched laugh that made him smile, then the words kept coming out. 'I don't normally ask my customers, it's none of my business who they're for, could be anyone- girlfriend, aunty, girlfriend. Anyway, yes, no problem, let's have a look here. Are you flashing your cash again? Oh sorry, I totally didn't mean that either, it was very generous of you to spend what you did and obviously for my benefit too ...' I grinned at him through gritted teeth. 'I'm going to stop talking.'

'I like it when you talk.' His smile was genuine.

Was he flirting with me? He'd admitted later it had been hard not to. There was a silence and I really didn't know what to say, so I bombarded him with the treatment list again.

'Look,' he'd stopped me, enabling me to meet his eye, 'I've got a confession to make.'

'You're not gay, are you?' OMG! I was booking myself in to have my mouth sewn up.

'No!' He seemed surprised. Not that there was anything wrong with being homosexual, but he'd be no use to me if he was.

'Sorry, I think I have a mild dose of Tourette's.' Oh God, why couldn't I shut up? Now it looked as if I was poking fun at people with difficulties. I wasn't, I promise; we raised money for charities. My salon contributed, I promise. I took toys to the hospital at Christmas, donated through the salon. I'd tried to run a three-mile fun-run. I did try, I promise. My legs wouldn't take me. My body wasn't made for running; it was made to pamper others, not put myself through torture.

'I need a voucher for a massage, or something like that.'

'Oh!' Obviously, I'd scared him off making his 'confession'. He admitted to me later that he'd found me so endearing that he'd lost his nerve when I'd asked if he was gay. I remember that I'd caught my breath and tried not to say anything that might stop him buying the voucher. I'd held my tongue and pretended he wasn't so gorgeous, his tempting, clean aftershave nibbling at my nostrils, his sweet breath close as we analysed the type of massage he was interested in. He decided on a back massage.

Then he left; walked out of my life.

Again.

I'd rung Suzy, proceeded to tell her answer machine that 'I'd totally messed up my life.' Although I was talking to fresh air, I'd felt better once I'd admitted aloud that I was actually incapable of holding together any form of human relationship, especially with a man. I needed to be taken back to basics. I was thinking of joining a week's residential on how to communicate and not offend the world. Either that or plan B: a surgeon would stitch up my mouth.

***

Suzy still had the recording, tortured me with it every now and again. I thought about how different I was from Gina. I couldn't imagine her embarrassing herself; she seemed so together. Max had told me he loved that about me; the part that would let go and not worry what others thought. I couldn't imagine Gina being so laid back. Not that I'm horizontal but her anxiety about everyone knowing she was seeing Joe had been very apparent. Thoughts of our differences made me feel better, as did my focus on me and Max. The way we'd met, what he loved about me.

Maybe everything would be okay.

I tried not to focus on the conversation we would have tomorrow evening, I tried not to focus on poor Suzy, drowning in her nightmares, Libby, who was probably high on some illegal substance, or Dad, who'd probably passed out hours ago. Guilt gnawed at me that I'd not been to see him.

I tried to get all those negative thoughts from my mind, shift them aside as I fixated on the good things, all the things I'd achieved, how lucky I was, how grateful I was; but it was hard when this time tomorrow night Max would know that I wasn't that laid-back person he'd fallen in love with. He would know he had the potential to be a dad.

But I wasn't sure I could make that possible.

10

The third time I saw Max I was looking out the window, waiting for my next customer, who was running late. I gazed at the sparkling lights that bordered the windows, each small pane of glass edged with fake snow. Melanie was waxing in the treatment room; it was nice to have five minutes to watch and think; just be.

I was appreciating my own existence. I had these moments sometimes. My salon was perfect, the cosy abode was mine. It was all I'd wanted to make Mum proud. It was snugly situated in Great Ayton, where the small stony river and ice-cream parlour added to the enchanted, picturesque setting. The view out of the salon always stunned me. The river backed onto where we were, and it was possible to see the ducks. In the summer, it was lovely to watch the kids feeding them; when the door was open we could hear the hilarity of young voices. This particular day was calm; somewhat soothing. There was a low wind, each flurry of air swinging through the leaves quietly, with only a whisper. I focused on the oak tree which stood protectively over the river, my thoughts deep in places where I didn't venture too often.

The sound of the door chime wrenched me back. Realising my customer had arrived I pulled myself quickly from the chair.

But it wasn't my late customer; it was Max.

I'd pushed thoughts of his attractiveness from my head, in case a Freudian slip jumped out. His smile was sheepish, almost apologetic. I'd doubted I see him again. He'd left it a few weeks, so I thought I'd scared him off. I wondered who else he could possibly be buying vouchers for.

'Hello.' I smiled, greeting him like we were long-lost friends. 'What brings you here today?'

'More vouchers.' He rolled his eyes.

'For your mum?'

'Yes. She loved all her treatments so I was thinking I should get her a top-up for the New Year. I was passing and—'

'Look, Maxwell, isn't it?' I was surprised at how calm I felt; I wasn't turning into a gibbering mess like I had at our previous encounter.

'Max.' He blushed. Was he embarrassed that I knew his name? Or that this mother called him by his 'proper' name? It was hard to tell.

'Max, I don't mean to be rude, but—'

'Oh, God, was she awful? Are you barring us from your salon?' He was cringing.

'No.' Yes, she was hideous. 'But, I think your mum was expecting a little bit more than a backstreet salon.'

'She said that?'

'Not in so many words.' Yes, she said those exact words.

'Oh, God, I'm so sorry, you must think her a right snooty bitch.'

'No.' Yes, she was bloody horrible. 'She was fine.' I couldn't bring myself to lie too much; words such as 'lovely' and 'pleasant' wouldn't roll off the tongue.

'She wasn't. I know her.' He looked pained. I felt sorry for him. 'Please let me make it up to you.'

'Don't be silly. You paid for the vouchers. We're even.'

'Please let me take you out.'

'What?' I smiled. 'But I may have to meet your mum again!' OMG, why did this keep happening when he was around me? 'I'm sorry, that was a joke. I'm not sure why my brain doesn't engage—'

'Tourette's?'

'Err … something like that.' I could feel my cheeks burning, again.

'My friend has Tourette's.' His face was serious.

I couldn't think what to say. 'Sorry' seemed like a pathetic way to move this forward, so the words, 'Oh, right,' came out instead.

'No, not really. Sorry, I'm joking.' He smiled, but nervously as if testing how I would react to his humour.

'God, you had me worried. What are you trying to do to me?' Give me a heart attack, I wanted to add, but knowing my luck his bloody grandma had probably recently died from one.

'I'm trying to ask you out on a date, like I have for the past month.'

'The past month?'

'Yes, I was going to call in so many times,' he smiled. 'I'm crap at this.'

'So, what's different about today?'

'Well, my mum's upset you.'

'What?' I laughed, louder than I meant to. 'Do you really want to take me out on a date or is this all about your mum?'

'Oh Jesus, not a good start.'

'Not really,' I said.

'Right, let's start again … Kat—'

'You know my name?'

'Yes, Mum told me. She hates it when people shorten their names.'

'I thought we were starting again.'

'Yes, sorry, forget my mother, Kathryn.' He winked at me, teasingly. 'Please can I take you out? Somewhere special, somewhere nice, because I want to, not because I have any other reasons but because I would like your company. Please.'

'Nah.'

'Really?' He reeled backwards.

'Sorry, I'm joking. I'd love to go out with you.'

Our sense of humour was only a small part of how we'd bonded.

***

I pushed these memories aside. I had to focus on the here and now. Max was coming to take me out for a meal and I was going to tell him about the baby. He wanted me. I had to tell myself this. He wanted me; not Gina. But would he want our baby?

Before I left I spoke to Marianne on the phone about Dad and promised I would visit tomorrow after work. I felt guilty. I also rang Suzy, who'd ventured home earlier that morning, cancelling all her appointments that day to 'veg on the sofa'. I hated not being able to help her. But when I spoke to her she was fine. The tears had stopped and she was planning her week ahead. Focused, as always. Although hurting inside, she wouldn't let the world see that. She told me Michael had sent her a text telling her he was sorry and could they arrange the next session. She'd sent one back telling him she would no longer be his personal trainer and hoping he would find someone to replace her soon. Always the diplomat. I'd have phoned him screaming, shouting and demanding answers, regretting my actions later. I was proud of her for holding it together and calmly telling him where to go.

Libby was my last call, but she'd not answered. I didn't bother to leave her a message, as all I could think to say was, 'Just making sure you're okay,' which we both knew meant, 'I'm checking up on you.' She was an adult living her own life in her own way. I had to try and accept this.

Max was fifteen minutes early. Luckily, I was ready. Dressed in black trousers and a black top that floated elegantly around my waist, I'd purposely chosen an outfit that would hide the bloated effect this pregnancy seemed to be having on me.

'You look gorgeous.' He kissed my cheek as we hugged, his closeness filling me with satisfaction and warmth.

'I'm sorry,' I said. Although we'd made up on the phone I needed him to know I was glad he was here.

'I'm sorry too.' He kissed me softly and I knew we were okay.

For now.

He drove us to the venue that he'd first taken me to. I smiled at how romantic and thoughtful he was. The Olden Arms was a country pub that was situated in the fields, winding roads leading to its secluded location. When we'd first visited, the fire had been roaring and the owner roasted chestnuts for his customers. The low beams, the authentic red décor and old wooden furniture made all the customers feel cosy.

When we arrived, he suggested we sit outside with the evening still being so warm.

There was another couple admiring the scenery.

We sat some distance away from them. Not because we were unsociable, but because they seemed to be enjoying the tranquillity and we wanted to do the same.

We ordered our drinks and he looked at me suspiciously as I enjoyed a lime and lemon rather than the usual wine I would have chosen. 'Are you still not feeling right?'

'I'm okay. Well actually …' I paused and took a sip of my drink, my mouth dry, anxiety running through me as I thought about how the words would sound.

'You're not right, are you? It's all this stuff with Gina and my mum, isn't it? Look, I've told you there's nothing between me and Gina anymore.' He seemed frustrated but didn't raise his voice.

'I know it's over. I was being silly and obviously with her seeing Joe now—'

Max's face changed to one of either misunderstanding or disappointment, 'Joe?' he asked, obviously trying to hide whatever reaction he was feeling. 'As in, my Joe?'

'Yes, your Joe. I thought your mum would have told you.' I felt myself tense at his response to this news. 'Anyway, I thought there was nothing between you two, so why do you look like I've told you someone's died?'

'Don't be silly, Kat,' he said, becoming agitated. 'I'm not bothered about her, but I don't understand why Joe hasn't said anything.'

'Apparently, they wanted to see how it would work before they announced it.'

'Well, how come *you* know, but it hasn't been announced?' He seemed irritated that he was the last to know but I couldn't help wondering if it was Gina that was bothering him.

'Well, Paula announced it in the salon yesterday. Gina seemed a little unhappy that she had, and your mum seemed extremely put out that she didn't know.'

'I bet she did!' Max laughed, seeming to find some form of amusement in this.

'Gina came back in and told me she was happy with Joe.'

'Well, I'm pleased for them, but I can't believe he didn't tell me.'

'Does he have to tell you everything?' I tried to make light of the situation but it sounded as if I was having a dig.

'Dating an ex is usually information shared.'

I tried to imagine Suzy dating one of my exes', how upset I would be if she'd not told me. I could understand Max feeling saddened by Joe's inability to share his life with him. Suzy missing out such a crucial piece of information just seemed implausible, but maybe I knew that wouldn't happen as the few men that I'd dated were not spectacular, if anything I wondered why I'd dated them myself.

'Are you bothered?' I asked him directly not wanting to play mind games.

'Of course not.' He shook his head, placing his hand over mine. 'Not at all. I hope they're very happy. I'm just surprised that Joe never mentioned it. I see him nearly every day. Anyway, let's forget about them.'

I had to believe him.

But my need to tell him about the baby had lost its urgency. His concern for his ex, although he was telling me it wasn't her that bothered him, and I somewhat understood, still this broke through my thoughts, no matter how I tried to push it away. I didn't want him worrying about Joe and Gina, or Gina and whoever she was with.

He'd always been loving, kind, true and attentive, and he was still those things, but I felt a loneliness that I'd never experienced with him before.

I knew I had to tell him about this baby, but now I couldn't summon up the words.

As we worked our way through our meals, we talked lightly about the amount of training he'd been doing. Lawrence and Joe were putting in as much time and effort as he was. He was surprised Joe had time for Gina. There she was again!

Her name struck me hard; my insides felt the weight of an indescribable burden. It was Clare who'd first told me about their relationship and how happy the families had been.

And now I felt threatened by this pretty, stunning woman. I knew I could play the pregnancy card, make Max commit to me. But I didn't want to do that.

I wanted him to want *me*, not because I was having his baby.

We drove home pretty much in silence. Max asked if I wanted to go back to his house, but I asked if it would be okay to come back to mine. We usually only stayed at his on Saturday nights when I could enjoy his huge super-king bed, not having to worry about the effort of waking to serve my customers.

Suzy would often ask, 'Why does he stay with you? Why waste all that space?' To say that Max's house was bigger than mine was an understatement: being an architect, he'd designed it himself. It had five bedrooms, three bathrooms and a hot tub. My small, two-bed abode would fit into a quarter of his downstairs. But I didn't care. It was my home.

Gina had lived with Max in his house for a couple of years, I believe; I've never asked the number of years. But now I wanted to know exactly when they'd got together, how they *really* split up (had they simply grown apart?), what words were used in the deciding factor that they should no longer be together, what feelings and emotions were formed? Plus, what happened after that? Suddenly, there were a whole load of unanswered questions that unsettled me to my core; firstly, because I'd met her and she was lovely, and secondly, because the life of this baby could be affected by this whole scenario.

I forced myself to think about how Max and I had met. How we were meant to be together. How I'd been wary of Clare from day one, but still I wanted to see Max. I fell in love with him despite the tension I received from his mother, so why should Gina be any different. And the fact of the matter was she'd moved on. She was happy.

Later, as I watched him sleep in my bed, his breath soft and quiet, I knew I was being silly.

His eyelids flickered. He was obviously dreaming, I wondered about what? Gina?

I *had* to stop this. I was going to drive myself insane. He'd told me it was me he wanted. He had said those words over and over again. If I didn't listen, I would push him away.

I snuggled next to him so I could feel his breath upon my face. As I closed my eyes, I decided I would definitely tell him in the morning.

<h1 style="text-align:center">11</h1>

When I awoke I realised immediately that he wasn't with me. He had been replaced by a small note that sat upon my pillow with a teddy that he'd bought me months ago. His handwriting was usually scruffy, a fast scribble that I often found hard to read but this was clear: *Had to go. Running with Lawrence and Joe. Love you, will call you later. Yours forever xxx*

The note made me smile, filling me with tenderness, but at the same time I wanted to scream. I really wanted to tell him. The urge was so overwhelming, I'd nearly woken him in the night. Now wishing I had, I picked up my mobile phone. There was a text.

I do love u xxx very much xxx

He'd sent it at 5.45a.m. He always trained early if he was working. It allowed him to get home for a shower, then in the office for 8 a.m.

I love u 2 xxx very much xxx

My reply seemed flimsy compared to what I wanted to say. But a text or a phone call wasn't sufficient for this announcement. I sent him another text asking him if he could come over that evening and he replied that he could.

So tonight it would be.

There would be none of this talk of Gina or letting other thoughts get in the way when he arrived. My plan was simple: I would sit him down before offering any drinks and tell him the news. 'I'm pregnant.'

I practised aloud as I watched my mouth move in the mirror. 'I'm with baby,' 'I'm having a baby,' 'We're having a baby,' 'I'm up the duff.'

Still struggling to work out which phrase rolled off my tongue the easiest, the last one probably not the best, I pulled back my mane of lacklustre locks, added bronzer to my washed-out skin and wondered what people meant when they talked about 'the glow'. Glowing in pregnancy, I decided, was a fallacy. I'd seen many pregnant women over the years of doing treatments. Most complained of tiredness, sickness in the beginning and feeling completely fed-up. Don't get me wrong, there were women that bloomed. But I wasn't sure there were that many. I'm generalising, I know, which I hate doing, but I'll be honest, I didn't get it. Glowing, blooming, feeling sexy and horny … *really*? I couldn't imagine feeling erotic ever again.

I worked on making my face look a hell of a lot better. I used to thank my training in beauty when I had a hangover. I felt slightly gutted that I looked and felt so bad without the pleasure of having a drink. Thinking of drinks, I remembered I must talk to Suzy about her birthday, so I send her a text to ensure she was sticking with her plan today.

I'm fine just gettin ready 4 1st client, did u tel Max? x

So about yor b'day, shal we do Tues? Out 4 dinner. x

R u changin subject? U didn't tell him!!! x

Promise, 2nite. Yor b'day??? x

Tues, dinner, gr8. X

8pm x

Fab x

Fab, will book 2day. X

As soon I was in the salon I made a note to reserve a table at Central Park, her favourite restaurant. Melanie was preparing the treatment rooms, Sophie hadn't arrived in yet. I could hear Melanie singing to herself. She was always full of energy. Her exercise regime with Suzy had seemed to boost her to a different level. Not only had her figure changed, but her confidence and joy for life. She put me to shame at the moment.

'Mel, I've been thinking about employing someone else. What do you think?' I raised my voice so that she could hear me.

She stopped what she was doing and came to talk to me. 'I think it's a great idea.' I wasn't sure if I heard relief in her voice. 'But can you afford it?'

'Well, I'm sure I'll manage.' I tapped my pen on the diary. Names had been squeezed into nearly every space. We were both fully booked every day. I should have thought about this earlier. But Max had come into my life like a whirlwind. I'd lost my business focus, not working strategically but fire-fighting, which was a bad way to run a business. I'd done enough training to understand 'eye on the ball, always'. 'Just someone part time for now, do you think?' Melanie agreed with me. 'Right, I'll ring around some of the colleges and see—'

'Do you know my friend Mandy?' Melanie interrupted me. I nodded, vaguely remembering a name that had been mentioned in the past. 'Well, she's qualified. She's worked in a few places and is now sort-of working for herself but I know she wants a job rather than being self-employed.'

'Great, let's get her in for a little interview, if she's interested.' It would be good to hire someone that one of us knew. I needed people I could trust. You couldn't always tell from interviews. Sometimes the college would make recommendations, but usually all the CVs looked the same. I needed personality and charisma; someone who would connect with the customers.

Melanie was on her mobile to Mandy as the salon phone rang. It was before 9a.m. and usually we let it settle on the answering machine but the excitement of making our small team bigger had sparked a small light of energy within me.

'Soothing Salon, how can I help you?'

'Morning, you.' It took me a second to recognise Max's voice. He didn't normally ring on the salon phone. He knew how busy I was when I was here, so if he needed me he would leave me a message on my mobile.

'Morning. What are you doing ringing this number?'

'Surprising you.' He laughed at his own joke.

'Sometimes, Mr Shields, you are quite dorky.' I smiled, loving his silly sense of humour. 'How was the run?'

'Great. I'm knackered but it was great. Just off to the office and thought, best ring you quickly about Saturday night.'

'Saturday night?' Had I forgotten we had arrangements? Quickly racking my brain, I couldn't think of anything.

'Yeah, well, I asked Joe about him and Gina. He wondered if we'd like to go out for a meal with them on Saturday night.'

'And you said?'

'Well, I'd ask you, of course.'

'But if I say no, then it looks like it's me that has a problem with them.'

'Do you have a problem with them?' He seemed dismayed by my response.

'No, it's just … Gina's your ex, and isn't that going to be awkward?'

'No, I've told you, me and Gina are over. Joe's my friend. If he had a different girlfriend we'd be out with them all the time.' Would we?

'Great then, get it booked.' The falseness in my voice either fooled Max or he chose to ignore it.

Gina again.

I was trying to keep her at the back of my mind but she kept whacking me in the face like a bloody great brick. I imagined Joe and Gina having the same conversation. Would she want to come? Would she feel the reluctance I felt? Why would she want to come out with us?

This was a nightmare. This woman who had so many shared memories with my man wouldn't get out of my life; bloody Gina, with her bloody prettiness, bloody niceness. I told myself it was all in my head. Gina was with Joe, not with Max. I *had* to believe this, because I knew I couldn't bring a baby into this world without Max's support.

The more Gina was bashing me with that brick, the more I knew there would be no baby.

12

The day went quickly. The salon was full of women chatting, relaxing and enjoying being in my safe haven. I loved the atmosphere that brimmed with laughter and satisfied customers. It made the stress of running the business worthwhile. Melanie had organised for her friend to come for an interview the following Monday, as we couldn't squeeze her in this week.

As I drove to Dad's house after work, I thought about my salon. It felt amazing that we were moving it forward. Employing another person meant we were going in the right direction. It was lovely to feel positive about something in my life.

I was holding onto it like a safety rope.

I arrived at the house where I'd lived for many years after Mum had died. Dad had lost our other house: once he'd lost his job he couldn't pay the bills and it had been repossessed. I don't think he knew I was aware of this, because he didn't tell me: I'd found the paperwork.

I pulled my car half onto the pavement and stared at the front of the house, searching for a sense of what was happening inside. The downstairs curtains were open, upstairs were shut. Perhaps he was having some quiet time in the bedroom, or maybe they were closed because he couldn't be bothered to open them. Shabby, unkempt brickwork stared back at me. The dirty white windowsills where paint had come away were thickened in areas by a green and brown, mouldy moss. Moss was also growing from the gutters. Dampness surrounded the whole house.

The houses to either side were nothing to be desired, either. The houses on Dad's side of the road all had gardens; not that anyone looked after them. Dad's was overgrown and although Max had offered several times to cut it, I'd said no. That type of thing would cause hell. If Dad was sober (okay, in between states of complete drunkenness, which is the nearest he got to being sober) it would upset him because he wasn't capable of doing it himself; then he'd drink more. A vicious circle that wasn't worth instigating; his moods fluctuated enough without any help.

I knocked quietly on the door before I entered, letting myself into the drab hallway. Wallpaper was torn in obscure places, black marks added to the old-fashioned pink-and-yellow-flowered pattern, whilst the carpet, threadbare and dirty, had obviously been vacuumed at some point that day. The aroma of dinner filled my nostrils, which made me question if I was in the right place: Marianne once told me she didn't cook 'proper dinners' on an evening for her and Dad. There was no point, she'd said, he was ungrateful and didn't eat it. Chips and pizza was all he'd have. But the photos which hung diagonally up the stairs wall told me I was in the right place. Libby and I smiled back from them. Many of the photos had been taken before Mum died, and portrayed the perfect family happiness. It was Marianne who had made this shrine to me and my sister; it was Marianne who'd not included any photos of Mum.

'Hello, pet.' Marianne stepped from the kitchen, dressed smartly as always. An apron covered the neat, pale-blue skirt and white blouse; her fair hair was styled in a neat bob. She never had a hair out of place and I wondered who she made the effort for, because Dad didn't take much notice. Perhaps she did it for herself. Another part of Marianne I'd never asked about. She had a few friends from church that she talked about often, but they didn't visit. I imagined she was ashamed of Dad. I often wondered why she'd stayed around. Dad didn't offer her anything and Libby and I didn't give her much love. Why she'd chosen this life was beyond me.

'Hiya, is Dad okay?' This was always my first question.

'He's fine; he's in the living room.'

'So, he's up?' I whispered, smiling.

She nodded, smiling back at me.

'Living room' was an appropriate term to call the room that Dad *lived* in. I wasn't sure I'd seen him in any other place except this room and his bedroom. The bedroom was the place he would sedate himself when the days became too bad. He had diazepam on prescription. I'm sure he took more than his allowed dose, and added to his alcohol intake it would knock him out for hours (sometimes days). He argued that this never happened, and Marianne was in control of his medication, but when she left him alone (the church and shops being the only places she frequented) I wondered if he helped himself to more. He denied it.

He was sitting in his chair facing the television. A film displaying violence and gunshots blared from the screen. Dressed in old, baggy jogging bottoms and an ill-fitting black T-shirt he looked scruffy but he had shaved, which showed he was having a good day. Sometimes he went weeks without touching his razor. Although Marianne offered to do it for him, he would tell her to leave him be.

'Hi, Dad.' I kissed his forehead, taking in the sweet smell of soap. He didn't use deodorants, lotions or aftershaves. Marianne left them in the bathroom but he never made the effort.

'Hi, pet.' He seemed pleased to see me but didn't stop his film.

'How you doing?'

'Okay, pet.' He nodded, picking up the can of lager next to him. 'Do you want one? There's plenty in the fridge.'

'I'm okay thanks, Dad.' I watched him gulp down the fermented beer, wondering how many he'd had. Four? Five? He usually started with lager, finishing at some point with vodka or gin. We didn't mention it, though, as it only caused an argument.

When I lived with them, I would hide all the alcohol but he'd soon become aggressive, withdrawal making him quick to snap. He'd then storm out to the local off-licence. It was an endless cycle of quarrelling and battling. I once said to him, 'If Mum could see you now, she'd be disgusted.' He'd told me to leave the room. I later heard him sobbing to Marianne, but we arose the next day and all was the same. It was pointless. Marianne had tried to get him help, but he wouldn't accept it.

'What's the film?' It was small talk; I couldn't ask what he'd been doing as I knew the answer was nothing.

'Dunno,' he shrugged, 'Not even sure I get it.'

'Well, put something else on.' I tried to laugh and he smiled vaguely; the most I would get out of him.

'Dinner's ready.' Marianne put her head around the door.

'Look, I'll leave you to it.' I stood up and made my excuses, not wanting to linger.

'I've made you dinner too,' Marianne said. 'Well, with Libby coming I thought it would be nice for us to sit down together.'

'Libby's here?'

'Yes, she's in the kitchen.'

I followed Marianne but really wanted to walk the other way and out the front door. Dinner? This was typical of Marianne. She knew that if she'd asked me first, I would have said no, I was busy. It wasn't that I was being rude, but I could only stay in their company for a short time before I felt as if I would crack. I hated playing happy families because we were far from that.

'What are you doing here?' I asked Libby, who was leisurely drinking a glass of wine.

'Visiting,' she snapped at me.

I hadn't meant to be so abrupt with her and was maybe a little provoked that she was visiting without my knowledge.

'Right, girls, isn't this lovely,' Marianne said, rather to herself than to us.

I sat down next to Libby. 'So, how's work?' I asked.

'Shit.'

'Libby, do we have to use that language?' Marianne piped up in the background. We both ignored her. We always had when she said anything with authority.

'Libby, you've got to stick this out, or at least find something else.'

'I know, so you keep saying.' She sounded like a defiant teenager. I felt like a strict mother.

Marianne placed plates crammed with food in front of us. Roast lamb, a mixture of vegetables, roast and mashed potatoes smothered in gravy.

'Jesus, Marianne, this could feed a family for a week,' Libby commented as my stomach turned at the thought of putting even a spoonful of the sloppy mess into my mouth.

I thought back to Clare's well-presented meal, her new potatoes with herb dressing and onion gravy made from scratch. The two dinners defined the line between mine and Max's upbringing. Marianne's roast potatoes were still rolling in fat, and the lumpy mash and the overcooked lamb with its burnt edges were the reason I never came here for dinner.

'I wanted you girls to be nicely fed. Brian, come on, your dinner is ready,' Marianne shouted into the hallway.

She placed his food next to mine, on the small round table which still had edged decorative marks where Libby and I had deviously carved out pieces with our knives and forks. The sun had faired the wood slightly, and stains where cups of hot liquid had been placed without coasters added to the tattered appearance. It was amazing that so many memories could be recalled from this piece of wood. Whilst I was studying the table, I felt Marianne's eyes upon me.

'You look a bit peaky, are you okay?' she asked.

'I think I've caught a virus or something, I've been off colour for days.' I wouldn't normally tell her how I was feeling, but I really couldn't stomach the heap on the plate in front of me.

'Well, this should help. Come on, eat up.' So that didn't work.

Dad came and joined us. 'Oh, this looks lovely,' he said to himself rather than to us.

I watched him as he moved slowly into his chair, resembling someone thirty years his senior. He was a tall man and when Mum was alive he had broad shoulders and a manly physique. His presence had been forceful but loving. Now he was weak. He had not an inch of fat on his bones and his gaunt features made him look unwell under the grey of his skin.

Marianne sat snugly next to Libby as she silently placed her hands together and said a small prayer. She didn't inflict grace upon us, and it was only in the last few years she'd started to appreciate something before she ate, or maybe she was begging for change. We respectfully waited for her to finish. Dad rolled his eyes and mumbled something under his breath.

'So, how's Max?' Marianne loved Max; 'A good boy,' she would tell me.

'He's fine.' I smiled.

'Do we have any new men on the scene?' She directed the question at Libby, who was scoffing her food as if she hadn't been fed for a week.

'Nah.'

Marianne continued to bat questions at us, her eagerness to enjoy this family dinner so apparent I actually felt sorry for her. She knew we'd probably never sit down like this again. I couldn't remember the last time we had. It was torture. The food was probably lovely, but I really was struggling. I picked around with a few bits, making my way through the over-baked carrots, wanting to make an effort as I knew she'd probably think I was being defiant.

Dad didn't speak, just made his way through his meal, and when he'd finished, which was before everyone, he burped loudly. Nausea swept over me even more strongly than it already was.

'You enjoy that, Dad?' Libby encouraged.

'Smashing,' he said, rising from his seat.

'Are you finished?' Marianne chewed some food as she looked up at him.

'Yeah, I'll just go and sit it off.' He patted his stomach, before rudely leaving the room. I picked at more carrots. Libby had practically finished off her plate and Marianne was eating elegantly, chewing every piece of her meat as if she wanted this moment to last a lifetime. I remember Mum never letting us leave the table until everyone had finished. It's incredible how one person can have so much influence in one's life; take that person away and everything from morals, opinions and beliefs are quickly altered.

'Marianne, I'm sorry, really I am, I've not been well,' I apologised, as I couldn't possibly twitch my fork around my plate anymore.

'Don't worry. You don't look well. It's just nice to have you girls here together.'

Libby poured herself another glass of wine. I realised she probably wasn't getting enough to eat. I wondered how she was coping, having to put food in the cupboards herself; the only time she'd shopped for us was with a huge list and my money. I hadn't minded. I loved having her with me, but I think she probably took most of her shelter and food for granted. Isn't that what most kids do with their parents?

I thought about this baby growing inside me. My ability to fend for another was evident in Libby, but did I really want to do it all again? Then there was the whole love thing. God, if I could bring Mum back tomorrow, how I would. How I would fight to have her with me. I'd heard many times, 'To lose a child is the worst thing. The parent is supposed to go before the child.' As I watched Libby, I couldn't imagine losing her. The fear shot through me like a bolt. Tears sprang to my eyes at the thought of not having her in my world.

'Kat, are you okay?' Marianne asked.

'I'm fine.' I waved a hand, dismissing my emotional behaviour. Bloody hormones. Marianne nodded at me. A knowing nod, as if she knew. She couldn't possible know. Suzy was the only person who knew and she wouldn't say a word to a single soul.

'Do you need a lift home, Lib?' I asked, wanting to shift the subject away from me.

'Oh yeah, great, if you don't mind?' If I did, she wouldn't have cared.

I made my excuses, explaining that Max was coming over. A nervous ball of tension rolled through my stomach as the words *I'm pregnant* sprang to my mind.

How would Max react?

If I'd been somewhere else, like Suzy's, I would have made every excuse not to leave. But being here made me claustrophobic. I didn't want to rush Libby but I really wanted to get out of here. Libby downed the last of the wine, after consuming a full bottle or so. Worryingly it didn't seem to touch her.

Marianne hugged us both, but as she took me in her arms she didn't let go. She kept me tight and I could smell her cheap perfume assaulting my senses and my stomach. Her big breasts squeezed against my hard, firm, sore ones. Her presence in my personal space was overpowering.

'You take care, Kat,' she said earnestly, as she finally released me.

I nodded, agreeing that I would.

'What the hell was that about?' Libby mumbled as we climbed into my car.

'No idea. Just smile, wave and let's get out of here,' I said under my breath, smiling at Marianne, who I hoped couldn't lip read.

We chatted a little as I took her home. Libby updated me on her housemates. She loved living with them; they simply wanted to party. 'It's like I haven't left uni. I love it,' she laughed.

'I don't mean to have a go, but life isn't one big party, Lib.'

'I often wonder, though: if Mum was here, would she agree with you?' She'd never pitted Mum against me before and I didn't like it. My memories of Mum were pure happiness. Of course, she would agree with me. Mum and I were very similar; we liked the same things and had the same interests. I couldn't imagine us ever falling out about anything. My memories held friendship, fun and laughter.

'The thing is, Kat, I have no idea what is around the corner,' Libby went on. 'I have no idea if I'll be here next week. If Mum taught us anything, it's to live our life.'

Libby was right. Pity she had to die to teach us this lesson.

As we turned into Libby's road, she was proved right; she had no idea what was around the corner. 'Oh shit,' she said. Two men were fighting on the pavement, one laying his fist into the other's stomach, the other swiping at his face. I slammed on my brakes as Libby jumped out of the car. I turned off the engine and followed her.

'Alan, Howard, for fuck's sake!' Libby screamed, trying to get in the middle of them both. Who the hell were Alan and Howard? I watched as Libby waded in, somehow avoiding the flying fists. Blood was dripping from one man's mouth. Finally, they parted.

'How the hell can you do this to me, Elizabeth?' The man who looked relatively fit started to cry; anger, frustration, helplessness, I wasn't sure. Elizabeth? No-one called her Elizabeth. Did she have some kind of secret life?

'Fuck off,' the man with the bloody lip shouted as Libby put her arms around him, telling him to calm down. I realised the street was full of spectators.

'I'll be telling your fucking wife,' the fit man shouted as he stormed off.

'Come on now, there's nothing to see here,' a young man told the neighbours, who had formed an audience. They mumbled words like 'disgusting', 'ashamed of themselves' and 'humiliation', but I thought this amusing as they were probably enjoying the excitement.

I recognised the young man; he was one of the housemates. He called himself Calvin. I didn't believe this was his real name. I didn't believe his parents would have named him that twenty-five years ago. All I got from Libby was, 'He's so much fun; he's an events manager, gets us into all the clubs, but you don't have to worry about me and him because he's gay.'

Libby had her arm around the injured man's waist as they walked towards the house. I shouted her name. She mumbled something to the man, who looked much older than her. He nodded and walked ahead into the house.

'What the hell is going on?' I demanded. 'Did *that* man,' I pointed in the fit man's direction, 'just say he would tell *that* man's,' I pointed at the house, 'wife?'

She knew me well enough to know my strong views on monogamy. I thought it must be dreadful to find out that the person you devote your life to doesn't devote theirs. I expected my partner to be faithful. There wasn't any compromise. It wasn't a rule that Max and I had put in place. It was an unspoken understanding. Don't get me wrong, I wasn't naive enough to think that all couples stayed in love forever. Sometimes circumstances prevented relationships from working. But I believed in true love. I liked to believe that if Mum had lived, she and Dad would have stayed together.

'Oh Kat, please don't start with your bloody morals now.'

'I'm not, I'm just asking.' That was a lie. I wanted to ask, how long has he been married? Let's talk about his wife, what does she do? What does she look like? Where does she think he is when he's shagging you? Does he have kids?

'His wife is awful to him.'

'Says who? Him?'

'Alan loves me.' She looked at me, obviously desperate for me to believe her. 'I love him. I was only seeing Howard for a few weeks. He's so possessive. It's such a mess.'

'You can say that again.'

'Look, I'm going to go and see if he's okay. Thanks for the lift.' She kissed my cheek and we hugged, before she rushed off inside, closing the door. I wondered, if I'd attempted to follow her in, would she have let me into her life? I realised as I walked back to my car that I knew nothing about my sister. We'd lived with each other for years as children, then she'd lived with me up until a few months ago; and I knew nothing about her. She had no concept of real life; her world was a bubble that consisted of Libby. People came and went; how she affected them was little to do with her, and there weren't many who could affect her.

My phone rang as I got into my car. I realised I hadn't sent Max a text to say I was leaving Dad's. He was probably expecting me over an hour ago. But it was Suzy's face with her tongue hanging out at me.

'Hiya, you okay?' I asked, starting my engine.

'I'm pregnant.'

13

Suzy looked as anguished as she had when she'd found out he was married. Mascara had become her new camouflage as it spread inelegantly across her face. I'd rung Max on the way home, explaining I had to go to Suzy's house. I didn't tell him why; not because I didn't trust him, but I needed to see Suzy first.

My own anxiety was rocketing; every time I went to tell Max about the baby, something got in the way. If it went on much longer, I'd have no choice but to have the baby. Not that I knew how far along I was or at what point the decision would be taken out of my hands.

Subconsciously, maybe this was what I wanted. No, that definitely wasn't the case. What I wanted was to believe there was no baby, that I was living someone else's life or that soon I'd wake up from a very bad dream.

I arrived at Suzy's three-bedroomed house. Her father had paid a hefty deposit for her, so her mortgage was pennies compared to most. She'd completely redecorated the house; her own stylish touch brought in a fashionable vintage theme throughout her home. Shabby-chic furniture filled each room, ornamental accessories enhanced the theme and delicate fabrics draped finely. Everything was staged; thought had been put into every embellishment and trimming.

She hugged me tight when I stepped over her threshold. Tears were streaming as she tried to catch her breath.

I sat her down on her neat sofa, which didn't have a cushion out of place. 'Right, tell me what's happened. When did you find out?'

'A few hours ago,' she sobbed. 'I've done something really stupid.'

'Oh my God, you've not told his wife?'

'No, but I should. He's such a bastard.' She sobbed again. This behaviour was so unlike her, I was unsure how to comfort her. It was usually the other way around.

'Does he know?' She nodded. 'Right, tell me from the beginning.'

'I was due on today.' She choked on another sob. 'I know I said I'm not always regular but I thought I'd get a test on the way home. I really thought it would be negative.' The word 'negative' set the tears rolling again. She tried to carry on talking but I couldn't understand what she was saying.

'Calm down, I'm not sure I get this. So, you did the test, you rang Michael and asked him to come round.'

'I didn't know what else to do.'

'He brought flowers and chocolates, you kissed, one thing led to another.'

'I'm so stupid.'

'You then told him and—'

'He was so awful. He said I must get rid of the baby. He said he would pay, he said if I didn't do something about it, then he would.' More tears escaped her as the sounds of heartbreak filled the room.

'Oh my God, Suzy.' I couldn't think of anything else to say. After hugging her close for a few minutes, I said, 'Let me put the kettle on.' I wasn't sure how a cup of tea would help at that moment, but my mouth was dry and I needed to think straight. I felt British when I said it, though. I'd read somewhere, it's only the British who thought they could solve all problems with a cup of tea. However, my usual problem-solver was a glass of wine. After the night's events, I could have murdered a glass but was worried I'd throw it back up.

Two cups of tea made, I was ready to analyse the next step. Ready to conquer the next chapter with her, although I wasn't sure what the next chapter involved.

'I want to keep the baby.'

'But he doesn't want anything to do with the baby.'

'I don't need him.'

'I know that, it's … well …' I didn't know what I was trying to say, but I didn't want her being hasty and making the wrong decision.

'Well what?'

'Well, he'll have to be involved. What if his wife finds out?'

'Seriously, Kat, that's a bit lame. I don't give a shit if his wife finds out.' She sounded like Libby. I could imagine Libby saying that, if I'd grilled her about the fight in the street that evening. It sounded odd coming from Suzy; like she'd been possessed. 'The thing is, Kat, men like Michael should be shot. I might not be the only person he's got pregnant. He could have kids all over the place. She probably hasn't got a clue.' Her tears had turned to anger; rage filled her words.

'I totally agree with you, Suz, I really do.' I didn't dare not. I didn't know how to deal with Suzy like this, which sounds odd when we've been friends for so long, but she wasn't an angry person. Nothing fazed her. She wasn't one to sweat the small stuff, she looked at the bigger picture; and now here she was, burning with resentment.

'I can't believe I slept with him again.'

'I'm a bit shocked.'

'I know, but he was so lovely, and then next thing I know, well, it was all over really before it started.'

I nearly choked on my tea. 'I can't believe you let it happen when you knew he was married though.' I felt my motherly side squeezing its way through, shouting for attention.

'Kat, I don't need a lecture,' Suzy snapped.

'I'm just saying, it's not like you.'

'Kat, bigger picture here. I'm pregnant with a married man's baby. Let's forget the sex thing, it's not worth talking about. You're supposed to be helping me, not judging me.' She looked sad and I felt a pang of guilt. She was right; although I wasn't judging her, it had sounded that way.

'I'm sorry.' I tried to smile. 'So, what are we going to do about this baby?'

'I've told you, I'm keeping it.'

'Are you really sure you want to?'

'I couldn't live with myself otherwise, Kat.'

'But it'll be so hard on your own.'

'I won't be the first or last single mother, I'll cope. It'll be fine.'

'I think you need to think this through.'

'Kat, it's this simple. I can't kill my baby.'

The words hit me like a shotgun. 'So, you think that's what I'm doing?'

'No, I didn't say that.'

'But you meant it.'

'I didn't mean it about you. I meant I couldn't live with myself if I had an abortion.'

'Kill my baby; your words, Suzy. Do you think I should keep my baby even though I'm not sure?'

'It's your decision, Kat, I'm just saying mine is to keep my baby.'

'But you're judging me.' I felt as if my heart was being ripped out. Suzy had never judged me before, she'd always supported me in everything. She gave me advice if I asked for it, and she'd find a solution to a problem; but she didn't judge me. She'd never made me feel like a bad person. Until now.

'Kat, I just think you need to look outside of your box. A baby could be the making of you.'

'It could also be the end of me.'

'How do you work that out?'

'I run a business, for a start.'

'So do I!'

'Well, it could interfere in so many ways. I haven't got a mother who will help out.'

'You have Marianne and Clare.'

'I wouldn't want them looking after my baby.'

'Kat.' Suzy breathed deeply as if exhausted by our conversation, running her hand through her hair and looking up at the ceiling, as if debating how to deliver her next words. 'You have so much love and support around you and you block it out with this hard exterior. Having a baby could be the best thing that has happened to you.'

'Suzy, don't pity me. A baby is not what I want. Having a child who may be snatched away from me at any time is not how I want to live my life. Look, I'm going to go.'

'Oh Kat, don't be angry.'

'I'm not angry.' I lied: I was fuming. 'But I don't want to get into this. I'm glad you're happy. I'm glad you have the confidence to bring a child into this world. I'm pleased for you.'

'Please don't go.'

'I've got work in the morning, and I'm shattered. Don't worry, we're fine.'

'Kat, I'm sorry, I shouldn't have said that.'

'You should; that's what friends do. I'm normally the opinionated one, though. I'm not used to it coming from you.' I forced a laugh, wanting her to know we were okay. But I needed to be alone. I couldn't analyse her life, my own life or anyone else's life. I needed some space.

'Are you okay?' I asked before getting up from the sofa.

'I feel great. It'll be a couple of weeks before any signs of sickness come along.'

'I meant, are you okay now? You know, with everything that's happened.'

'I'll be fine. I feel awful because I've upset you. You come to comfort me and I make you feel like crap.' Her eyes filled with tears. She bit her lip.

'You haven't upset me. I just didn't realise you felt so strongly.'

'About me.' Suzy seemed desperate for me to believe her. 'I've always wanted kids. Maybe not yet, but in a strange way I feel blessed. I don't need *him*. But, I need to know you're okay.'

'I'm fine. You're a step ahead of me, anyway; at least you've told the father.'

'I know. You really must tell him.'

I nodded. 'I will.'

14

Saturday arrived, yet still I'd had no opportunity to tell Max. He'd been training every night with Joe and Lawrence. The days seemed to pass without us having more than ten minutes together. Ten minutes wasn't long enough to tell someone something that could ultimately change their life.

Suzy's words haunted me, but I told myself she didn't understand. She'd apologised again and again throughout the week. She'd told me she really didn't mean it. We'd laughed about us both being hormonal and emotional. She'd hurt me. If my final decision went against what she thought I should do, where would that leave our friendship? I would know deep down that she thought I was wrong.

As I dressed in preparation for the meal with Gina and Joe, I chose black once again, to cover up the plumpness that was starting to surround my waist. I'd felt nauseous all day, more so than usual. The thought of joining Gina and Joe was too much. I thought about telling Max I was too ill, but Gina would know I was lying. I had no idea what the future held at that moment and if we were to become friends, although that idea filled me with dread, I needed to make an effort from the start. It would be the first time I'd seen Gina and Max together. I already had images floating around in my mind, torturing me. This would be reality. I'd be watching them for eye contact, affection, awkwardness. It was going to be awful.

Max picked me up, as always, on time. I wasn't sure whether this was natural for him, or because I'd harped on about lateness being the height of bad manners. I wasn't going to analyse it, though, as I enjoyed his ability to be there when he said he would be.

I thought about telling him on the way there but the words stuck in my throat, as if a blockage held them back. It was a good thing, as we'd probably not have made it to the meal. No, I would tell him when we arrived back at his house. I was looking forward to our Saturday night in his luxurious bed, our Sunday morning lie-in and his gorgeous cooked breakfast.

Gina and Joe held hands as they walked towards us, Joe grinning. His smile was infectious. He had a cheeky grin that made him look about five years old. He was what I would describe as *cute*. I'd never really gone for cute men.

'Now then, mate.' He held out his hand to Max, who shook it. Joe leaned in to give me a hug. He smelled clean, with a hint of aftershave. Gina hugged me too, her smile reaching her eyes, lovable and warm. Gina and Max then hugged, as I watched intently for a hug that was too long, too short, too awkward, too over-familiar, too … I don't know, too *something*. There seemed to be nothing; they were comfortable, but not overly. There was no awkwardness. An outsider would have thought we were all friends; a foursome that frequently went out together.

A waiter showed us to our table, as he would any other group of friends. I felt as though we had a neon light following us, an arrow above each of us, indicting what part we played. Was I really the only one who felt completely uneasy?

'Right, wines: shall we get a few bottles between us?' Joe asked, looking at the wine list.

'Sounds good,' Max agreed.

'Kat, is there anything you like in particular?'

'Oh, I'm driving.'

'What? Get a taxi home.' The thought of a night out without drink seemed completely alien to Joe. To be honest, a few weeks ago I'd have totally agreed with him.

'I've been off-colour so it's best to stay away from it, I think.' I smiled, trying to get him to focus elsewhere rather than on my drinking habits.

'Are you still not right?' Gina asked, remembering the comment Melanie had made in the salon. I could kill Melanie.

'I've told her she must go to the doctor,' Max said.

'I've made an appointment for next week,' I lied. This lying malarkey was becoming quite the norm.

My stomach was churning all the way through the meal. Delicious braised lamb shanks covered in fresh rosemary, garlic and red wine sat in front of me. I wasn't enticed by the smell or the taste. I picked my way through my food, eating small pieces, feeling stupid because I hated it when people were picky and wouldn't try new foods. I loved my food. My hips could back me up on that. But tonight, as for the past weeks, the nausea and anxiety were too overwhelming.

'Is it not nice?' Gina asked sympathetically.

'It's lovely, but I'm not that hungry.' I smiled. She smiled back knowingly. I wasn't sure what she thought she knew, but I appreciated her not carrying on this conversation.

Max and Joe talked about the Ironman contest, laughing about some of the men who would be participating with them. They talked about Lawrence, who was really offended he hadn't been invited out tonight. Both Gina and I agreed he could have come; he'd didn't have to have a date. Maybe next time, everyone agreed.

There would be a next time?

However, as the meal went on I felt a bit better about Max and Gina. There seemed to be no love between them: well, not in a sexual way. No passion or yearning for each other.

Until the desserts were finished.

Joe had downed a bottle of wine to himself, apparently a usual occurrence. His boyish grin was shining through as he leaned back in his chair, his arm around Gina. His dark hair had been styled to perfection. I could tell by the way there were some wisps to the side and some deliberately spiked to the top. In his younger days, I'm sure he could have been in a boy band. He had that endearing charm, an adorable expression that would melt the heart of any young girl.

Gina seemed to rise as he ran his hand down her back. She looked acutely uncomfortable as Joe said, 'We've got some news.' Both Max and I went quiet as Gina looked at Joe, smiling at him. 'We're getting married.'

'Wow, that's great news,' I said, after a pause that seemed to last for ever.

'That's amazing, mate! Oh God, what a shock. That's great news.' Max stood up to shake Joe's hand.

Then I saw it. I saw that look between Gina and Max. A look of guilt, compassion, concern, empathy … I don't know, but it was there. Gina looked remorseful, her eyes seemed to be pleading with Max, who hugged her close. Congratulating her. Max's eyes seemed glazed by regret. I don't know; it was a second. It was a flash, a moment.

But it was there.

My heart plummeted to the bottom of my stomach, as it dawned on me: he *did* still love her, he *must* still love her. Why else would he look so repentant? Had I imagined it? Was I looking for it? Why would Gina marry a man she didn't love? Marrying Joe would mean Max would be in her life forever, but their mums were friends so that would be the case anyway. My thoughts were racing as my world seemed to be crashing around me.

I excused myself and went to the Ladies. My throat ached with the need to give way to the tears. Had I really seen that look? Had I wanted to see that look? Was I so desperate for there not to be a connection, I'd imagined it? I didn't know. I needed some air.

I walked past the toilets and went outside into the warm summer night. I forced myself to breathe deeply, inhaling the fresh air, pushing back the tears. I hadn't realised how long I'd been standing there, trying to compose myself as thoughts collided each other, when suddenly I felt his arm upon my shoulders.

'Are you okay?'

'I'm sorry, I felt really sick.'

'Okay, do you want to go?'

'I feel rude, Max, but do you mind?' I would never normally have left an evening with friends early (if I can call them friends). I would never have left my companions sitting at a table wondering where I'd disappeared to. I was never one for dramatics. It was best to conceal one's emotions. I'd learnt to do this to perfection by working in the salon. My customers saw me as the bright, bubbly therapist who never had a problem to deal with. My life was full of happiness; a pretence, but I'd never let them think otherwise.

But at the moment I was falling apart.

Max was back with me, cuddling me close as we walked to the car.

I felt my shoulders tighten as anger surged inside me. He had looked at her in a way that I couldn't let go. 'You still love her, don't you?' I slammed the words into his face as he got into the car beside me. I started the engine.

'*What?*' Max's eyes widened and he shook his head as if I'd slapped him. I stared at him, waiting for him to answer. 'Don't be so stupid.'

'Stupid?' I put the car into reverse, the wheels spinning under my fierce handling.

Max winced at his precious car being treated so violently. 'I don't mean you're stupid,' he stuttered. 'Kat, please be careful with my car.'

I forced the gears as I manically drove away from the restaurant, forcing us back into our seats. Gravel hit the paintwork and Max sat tense, not moving or saying a word.

'I'm going to drop you off and go home,' I said, as I drove faster than the speed limit allowed.

'Please, Kat, there is nothing between me and Gina. I don't know how many more times I can say it.' His voice had become stern; it was obvious he was becoming angry with my theatrics.

'I saw you look at her. You were devastated.'

'I wasn't. You're being ridiculous. There is nothing between me and Gina. I was shocked; she and Joe have only been going out a few months. I thought it was a bit quick, that was all.' He sounded desperate for me to believe him.

It sounded viable, but I think I'd given up. I was tired of trying to think about what I should do, I was tired of wondering about this other woman, I was tired of trying to please everyone else and put this stupid grin on my face, to make everyone else feel better. I didn't want to do this anymore.

We arrived at his house. I could see the desperation in his eyes as he willed me to believe him.

'Kat, I love you.'

'Do you, Max?' I said, looking ahead. 'Do you *really* love me?'

'Of course I do, I don't know what you want me to do to prove it.'

'I shouldn't have to tell you.' My voice was low.

'Kat, please, you have to believe me. There is nothing going on between me and Gina.'

'I don't think there is anything going on. I think you both *want* something to go on. I think you both still love each other.'

'You're so wrong.' He ran his hands through his hair and breathed deeply. 'There is no me and Gina; we're friends. We ended it because it wasn't there, we had no connection. Not in the way I connect with you.'

I wanted to believe him but the look that had passed between them was sticking in my mind, torturing my soul. If I could have seen my heart, I imagined it crying with me, hurting from an ache it couldn't eliminate. I looked away from Max, studying his grand house, the place I should be staying.

'I need some space,' I whispered, as a tear escaped. I wiped it away quickly.

'Please, come in. I can't leave you like this. You've got to believe me, there is nothing between me and Gina.'

'But the way you looked at each other was—'

'I don't know what you're talking about. I was in shock. I don't care that they're getting married. I wish them every happiness. I want you. Please, Kat.'

'Max, I can't do this.' The tears ran down my cheeks, the saltiness filling my mouth. 'I didn't want to tell you like this, but you need to know.'

'What?'

'I'm pregnant.'

I watched his eyes fill with fear, shock, dread …

It wasn't happiness.

'Are you sure?' The panic in his voice was apparent. I nodded. 'Fantastic.' He seemed to mock his excitement, with an evident forced enthusiasm and lost boy expression.

Because of this, I knew what I had to do. 'I won't be keeping it.'

'What?' He turned hastily in his seat to face me.

'Your eyes tell a thousand stories,' I whispered.

'Please, stop with this whole 'how I look' thing. I'm telling you, this is *great* news. How long have you known? Is that why you've been feeling so ill?'

'Will you stop kidding yourself?' My voice was raised and I realised I was shouting at him.

'Calm down.'

'You could end up with me and a child for the rest of your life. A child isn't something you can pack off when you decide you're off on a jolly.'

'But I love you. I'd love our baby.'

'This is a huge decision.'

'We can do this together.'

'I need to go.'

'You can't leave now.'

'I need some space.'

I did. I didn't want to stay with him, analysing his feelings for Gina, working out whether he really wanted this baby, whether he really wanted me. I needed to think this through, quietly. Had I made all this stuff up in my head? The mind is so powerful, it has the ability to play unbelievable tricks. Had I been looking for something that wasn't there? Joe didn't seem worried about Max and Gina in any way, and he'd known them both longer than I had. He'd known them when they were together.

These thoughts whirled around as I lay alone in my bed. Max had tried to ring me a few times but I'd ignored his call. I couldn't think straight. I was hurting. My insides were being pulled in different directions; my mind was reeling with its own internal fight. He loves me, I told myself over and over again. He loves me.

But was that love strong enough? Could I really have this baby, suspecting that he loved someone else? He loved Gina, I was sure of it. I had no proof but something was stopping me from having this baby. Something deep within me was chewing at me, telling me to move forward on my own. Instinct? My own insecurity? My own emotional imbalance?

I was scared. I was terrified of having a baby, with or without Max. The gnawing sensation that was eating away at me was telling me what I had to do.

Max would probably hate me forever.

15

I stayed on the sofa all day Sunday. I'd excused myself from my weekly visit to Dad's. Marianne sounded concerned on the phone as she told me I really needed to see a doctor.

Max came and collected his car with his spare keys. He begged to come in, banged on the door, but I ignored him. I'd answered one of his calls and asked him to leave me alone. He respectfully agreed, although he'd texted me every hour since.

I hadn't told him my decision. I wanted to be alone, analyse things more, convince myself I would be doing the right thing. It was for the best, I told myself. I thought of Suzy and how she'd embraced this new life. I'd spoken to her on the phone, not mentioning that Max knew I was pregnant. I knew if I opened up to her she'd have been banging on the door, wanting to cheer me up; but it would have turned into a preaching session. I didn't want to be preached at. Suzy was enjoying this new stage in her life; the excitement was apparent in her voice. She didn't feel sick, whereas the waves of nausea kept coming at me like mini-hurricanes. Suzy had been reading books and magazines on how to be the perfect mother, how to look after your child from within the womb. She'd told me to eat. Eat! I couldn't face a thing. Every time I thought about food I wanted to throw up. She'd told me this feeling would go away. The books said this stage normally lasted for the first twelve to fourteen weeks. I didn't have a clue how far on I was, so this didn't really help me. Plus, I wasn't sure whether anxiety was the real cause.

By Monday morning, I knew these feelings had to be pushed aside. I couldn't allow my customers to see me like this. I made sure my face was flawless of any imperfections, my cheeks rouged and my eyes beautified from the large selection of shadows and pencils I kept in my bathroom. My mask covered me expertly.

Melanie had made sure we had no appointments first thing, so that we could interview Mandy. Her thick make-up and her mightily raised hair shocked me a little. Although both Melanie and I wore our foundations and blushers, we still maintained a natural look. We didn't look as if we had used a trowel to put it on. Mandy's thick eyelashes were obviously false, with at least five layers of mascara enhancing them. Her nails, artificially long, looked painful. I wondered how she could do a facial with those talons.

'It's so lovely to meet you.' She shook my hand and her softness surprised me.

'Thanks for coming in,' I said.

She took a seat on the sofa that was placed by the entrance for our customers. I sat on the reception chair and pulled it round to face her, hoping the informality of this meeting was obvious. I didn't want this to be an official interview with questions about her hobbies, strengths and weaknesses, and her trying to impress me. I wanted to find out about her, connect with her. If I could relax with her, I knew the customers would be fine.

She was lovely. I wanted to tell her she didn't need all the trimmings. I tried to tell her we ran a natural environment. I tried to say it in the nicest way without saying, 'You really need to tone down the hair. Wear one layer of make-up and lose the nails.' She nodded frequently, smiling continuously at me, agreeing enthusiastically. I liked her. Young, insecure and in need of a self-esteem boost, but I knew we could work on that.

It was agreed she would start on Saturday, three days a week to begin with. Saturdays were a given; it was our busiest day. In fact, we'd started to turn customers away.

I felt settled that one area of my life was now sorted. I no longer had to think about it. The diary would be managed and it would all fit into place. A trickle of excitement bubbled up: my salon was getting bigger. My dream was expanding. But the weekend's upheaval soon overtook me. I felt the nausea run through me like a rocky river, but the nausea I'd come to realise was actually not pregnancy related; well, maybe slightly, but it was the apprehension that squeezed my insides, grabbed at my heart and lungs, swirled around in my stomach, making me dizzy and breathless.

The phone rang and Melanie answered. I told her if it was Max, I was busy. She nodded, not asking questions. Lovers' tiff, she probably thought, totally unaware of how complicated my life had become.

'Kat, it's Libby.' Melanie handed me the phone.

'Thanks, Mel.' I took the phone from her. 'Hello, has your drama ended?' I said. I'd only spoken to Libby briefly since the incident outside her house. She'd told me all was fine. So I let her get on with it. I had my own troubles to sort out. I decided she was a big girl and must live her own life. I think what swayed me was the married man. My morals kicking in, I thought her behaviour too much to tolerate at the moment.

'I've been sacked.' Her indignation blared at me.

'Jesus, Libby!'

'It wasn't my fault.'

'It never is.'

'The bus was five minutes late so I ended up late for work, so he told me to leave and not come back.'

'You've been late every morning, haven't you?'

'Shit job anyway.' She ignored my question. 'Fuck 'em!'

'Is that any kind of attitude to have?'

'Well, they were all fannies anyway.' Her foul mouth never surprised me, although I'm sure our mum would have clipped her for it.

'Well, you better get searching for another job.'

'Yeah, I'll ring you later,' she said before hanging up.

The dramas of my sister, her laid-back attitude to life, amazed me. I knew she wouldn't look for another job, at least not for a few days. She'd be drunk or high or both for the next few days now. I thought about Dad. I wondered why she wasn't put off when she'd seen what drink had done to him.

Mrs D entered, her face full of smiles, her superiority a tangible presence in the air that surrounded her.

'Morning, Mrs Donnelly. How are we this morning?' Her name was Angela but she allowed no such informality. How I held back from calling her 'Ange', which is how her friends referred to her when they were in the salon, was beyond me. She was of similar age to myself, twenty-eight, give or take a few years, but I always felt as if I was addressing a school teacher.

'Fabulous.' She smiled, her whitened teeth gleaming back at me.

'Excellent, shall we do your nails first?'

'Oh please, I chipped one on the way back from Paris.'

'Oh dear.'

'I know, tell me about it. I was devastated. I tried to file it down, but I was so glad I had this appointment this morning, or I would have been ringing for an emergency one.'

'Lucky.' If that's all we had to worry about: chipped nails! How easy life would be.

'Am I with you this morning?'

'Yes, of course.'

'You're not letting that girl loose on anyone else, are you?'

'She's capable of doing a few treatments, she is qualified.' I wasn't prepared to join her in her put-down of Sophie. We've all got to start somewhere, which is what I'd told Sophie when Mrs D had left her in tears. I also relayed how I had once taken a customer's eyebrows off completely when I was training. (Well actually, I'd only taken one off; the other had to come off, as she looked rather odd with one eyebrow. I'd cried for days.) This poor woman was devastated, as it was her daughter's wedding, and my boss had to draw on fake eyebrows. My boss, a power-driven control freak and a horrid person with it, made me feel so bad, I vowed I'd never do that to my own staff.

'It was horrific, Kathryn,' Mrs D continued as she sat down opposite me at the nail station.

'I'm sorry, Mrs Donnelly, I really am. It was a mistake. Melanie thought Sophie had done lots of waxing before. She's so shy; she thought she was helping us. She was truly sorry and mortified.'

'There were patches all over the place. My Steve said I looked like I'd had a fight with a garden trimmer.' I coughed to conceal my laughter. Her face was serious, which made it worse.

'Right, let's look at these nails.' I changed the subject because I knew if I started to giggle, I wouldn't stop and I had to hold it in. Unprofessional, I know. I thought about the things I was trying not think about; the baby and Max. This soon put paid to my urge to laugh.

I worked on Mrs D's nails as she listed the endless restaurants they'd visited whilst in Paris. She talked about the clothes she'd bought, the money she'd spent, the places they'd visited. I nodded, smiled and laughed in all the right places. It was always so much easier when Melanie was in the same room, as she and Mrs D would share stories. Not that Melanie was anything like Mrs D in personality or dress and she certainly didn't have the money Mrs D had. But Melanie getting married was a subject Mrs D enjoyed. Love and happiness were all that life needed, she would say. I wondered if she would say that if her bank account didn't have as many zeros. Bobby had asked Melanie to marry him in Paris. I was starting to wish she was doing this treatment.

As I faked my interest in Mrs D's life, the door beeped. I assumed it was Melanie's next client, as I had Mrs D's pedicure to get through yet. The tables were situated behind a wall, so I couldn't see the entrance. Apologising to Mrs D, I looked around the divide, intending to tell the customer to take a seat. But I was faced with a pale, tired, unshaven Max. The nerves jangled inside me, my legs started to tremble.

I didn't need this now.

'Give me a second, Mrs Donnelly.' My voice was full of fake confidence.

'Kat, I need to speak to you.' His voice was shaking, and I felt my heart reach towards him.

'I can't do this here, Max,' I whispered urgently. I knew Mrs D would be straining to listen to every word.

'You won't answer my calls. What do you expect me to do?'

'I'll call you later.'

'I'll wait here until you're finished.'

'Max, please,' I begged him. 'Please let's talk outside.'

The hurt in his eyes tore at my heart, guilt flooding over me. He turned and walked out of the door and I followed him into beaming sunshine.

'Please don't do anything yet. We need to talk about this.' He was pleading with me.

'Look, I'll call you tonight.'

'Please do, Kat.'

'I will,' I whispered shamefully, mortified by the urgency in his voice.

He placed his hands on my cheeks, bringing my face to meet his. His soft lips were on mine, his tenderness enveloping me as he told me he loved me.

'We can do this, Kat.'

I nodded, and I watched him walk back to his car, guilt rushing through me. His vulnerability was endearing but I felt terrible that this strong character seemed helpless.

I'd made all of this about me. I'd not really thought about how Max would deal with it. I could see a huge issue with Gina that maybe wasn't there, I wasn't sure. But even if it *was* there, even if he did love Gina, who was I to make this decision on my own? I was wrong to think I could, although I really thought I was doing the best thing for both of us.

Mrs D was agog, asking me personal questions as if she actually thought I'd share my private life with her. 'The best thing about arguing is the making up,' she said.

I gave her my best smile, my customer-focused, bright, winning smile but inside I was crying. I was hurting. Max was hurting. It wasn't as easy as kiss and make up.

By the time I'd shut the salon, I was exhausted. I knew I had to ring Max. I knew I couldn't ignore him any longer. This wasn't about Gina and how he felt about her. This was about our baby. This was about our lives.

I collapsed on the sofa, my uniform clinging to me, the tightness on my waist obvious. I'd had to undo the top button of my trousers, surprised at how quickly my hips were expanding. I let out the tears which had been begging to be released all day. The emotions which were biting at me, the stirring, the swirling, the sickness, the inability to think straight, it was too much. I wanted to turn back time. I wanted to not only go back to the night this baby was made, but back sixteen years to when Mum was with me. I was sure things would be different, if she were here. I'd have probably welcomed a new baby in the family.

I imagined a happy life, with no loss or hurt to deal with. I imagined a life full of laughter, the way it was in Lampford Park. The way it was the day she died. As I spoke the words, 'Mum, what should I do?' tiredness overwhelmed me – I wanted this day to be over.

As I fell into a restless sleep, my phone call to Max not happening.

<h1 style="text-align:center">16</h1>

I awoke with a thick head, still on the sofa, dressed in my work attire from the day before. Oh God, Max. He was going to think I was avoiding him. I couldn't hurt him any more than I had already.

My mobile, which had been on silent, showed fifteen missed calls from him. Plus, there were five texts:

Where r u? We need 2 talk. M xxx

I've tried ringing 3 times, pls call me. M xxx

This is ridiculous, Kat, I need 2 talk to u.

I can't believe u r doing this 2 me. I don't think I no u anymore.

Wot the fuck r u trying 2 do 2 me? This is vicious. I shud hate u 4 puttin me through this. Who the fuck r u?

There was a knock on the front door. Was it him? But then I realised it was Melanie on her morning work-out with Suzy, red-faced, blotchy-eyed and looking like she'd been tortured, I let her in.

'She's going to kill me,' Melanie panted.

'And you pay her for it!' I smiled. I hoped she didn't realise I was still in yesterday's clothes. I let her use the shower first, thinking I'd jump in once she was downstairs in the salon. While she showered I picked up my phone and re-read Max's texts. The two last ones hit me hard. He *knew* who I was, but then, did I know who I was? I was struggling to find the person inside who could help me through this. Confident, bubbly Kathryn who brightened up the lives of others.

The word *vicious* stabbed at me. How dare he? I knew he must be angry, but did he really think I would ignore him when I'd promised I would call him? I felt my own anger filter through the despair. He obviously *didn't* know me. To be honest, he'd probably discovered that over the last few days; I knew he was shocked that I would even consider having a termination.

Most women would be thrilled to be in my position. Many would give anything, sell their soul to the Devil to have a child. I'd thought about these women who put themselves through rigorous and tortured treatments, such as IVF and more. Those who put themselves through the judging process of adoption. Having what they wanted made me feel guilty to my core for feeling so negative about my situation.

But what Max didn't understand, and I didn't know how to explain, was that Mum dying was the most horrendous experience. It was so incomprehensible it was difficult to put into words. The lost sense of reality gave way to a cold hardness that enabled me to partition off feelings and emotions I didn't want to face. Max wasn't aware I had this trait. It wasn't an evil part of me; it was like a secure place where I could feel safe. This may all sound cold, but it was how I dealt with Mum's death, how I'd lived each day, not analysing the hours, the minutes, the seconds she wasn't there. And it was how I'd been trying to deal with my pregnancy.

Melanie emerged from the shower, a pristine contrast to the sweaty figure she'd presented before. She went downstairs to open the salon, while I sorted myself out. She didn't ask questions; I appreciated her for this. I didn't want to open up to her; it was bad enough being judged by my best friend and boyfriend. I couldn't face it from anyone else.

I entered the salon to find Max waiting for me. I don't think he'd slept. He looked all-consumed, his eyes red, his face unshaven and ashen.

'Kat, we need to talk. You can't keep ignoring me like this.'

Melanie raised her eyebrows. 'I'll leave you to it,' she whispered, wandering into one of the treatment rooms.

'I'm sorry,' I said, walking towards him. 'I fell asleep.'

'How can you sleep at a time like this?'

'Well, actually I haven't been sleeping in weeks, so God forgive me if my body took over,' I snapped.

'We need to talk.'

'I know we do, but I can't talk now.'

'I'll meet you after work.'

'I can't. It's Suzy's birthday, we're going out for a meal.'

'Fuck Suzy's birthday!' His outburst shocked me and I stepped back from him. He seemed so desperate I didn't know how to handle him.

I realised my own anger had to be held back, as it wasn't going to help the situation. 'Look, Max, I've promised Suzy and I can't let her down.'

'I can't believe you're doing this to me.'

'I don't mean to. My head is all over the place. I can't think straight. I can't handle you coming in here shouting the odds.'

'What else do you expect me to do? You won't talk to me.'

I felt guilty that I was the cause of his pain. 'Look, we'll talk tomorrow. I promise.'

'But tomorrow's a bad day for you. I thought you'd want to be alone.' I was touched he'd remembered. With all this going on he'd actually remembered.

'I'll be fine,' I said, not knowing how I'd feel when I woke on Mum's birthday. In the beginning it was awful. I hated it. Dad was always at his worst around her birthday, so it had been a nice surprise to see how pleasant and together he was when I'd visited last week. But I had no idea how he would cope tomorrow.

'Right, I'll come straight from work.' His voice was softer and my body ached for us to be okay. I wanted him to take me in his arms, pull me close, hug me, tell me how much he loved me. He didn't today. He turned and walked away, not a kiss, not a goodbye.

I thought about how I'd been in awe of him six months ago, how my heartbeat had quickened and my hands had trembled. If I'd known what was going to happen, would I have been so quick to accept a date with him? Probably not.

Was our love strong enough to get us through this? I wasn't sure.

Melanie appeared as the phone rang. I wondered how much she'd heard.

'Soothing Salon, how can I help you?'

'I've been chucked out,' Libby sobbed.

<h1 style="text-align:center">17</h1>

Libby brought over her two suitcases of belongings. That was it. That was all she had to her name. As I worked, she settled herself back into her old room. Luckily I'd not moved anything, probably because subconsciously I'd known she'd be back.

I'd confirmed with Suzy that it would be okay for Libby to join us for our meal. Suzy as always was more than amenable and said that would be great, she'd not seen Libby in a while. It would be great to catch up. As I rang the restaurant to add Libby to our table, I knew I'd have to pay for her and the bottle of wine she would have to herself, but I didn't want her wallowing in self-pity. Well, truthfully, I didn't know who she might invite to the flat. I didn't want any performances like the other night. She needed to remember my salon was part of my home.

'Nice outfit,' I commented to Libby, who was wearing one of my dresses, ready for our night out.

'You don't mind, do you? All my stuff's crap.' As if she'd care if I did mind. She'd also helped herself to a glass of chilled wine. I didn't mind, but I knew it was going to be difficult with her helping herself to things and not contributing. When she was studying, it was different, as I knew she was working towards a good future and I wanted to help her. At the moment I didn't know what her plans were, but there was no way she was sponging off me. However, I thought we'd leave that conversation for now.

I could hear her chatting on her phone as I made myself look appropriate for the evening out; black attire covered me from head to toe again.

We picked up Suzy en-route to the restaurant. She was dressed in a bright pink top and skinny jeans, looking stunning with her blonde hair curled gracefully around her shoulders, her blue eyes sparkling. I wouldn't like to call it envy, but there was a part of me that wished I'd taken this news as well as she had. Her bright clothes showed her dazzlingly optimistic nature, whilst I was gloomily smothering my body with black layers. She had to be admired. I had a boyfriend who I could work through this with. She had no one. She hadn't told her mum yet. She knew she would have to tell her the whole story and although she hadn't known Michael was married, she wasn't sure how her mum would feel about her having a married man's baby.

We chatted as we drove, Suzy and Libby catching up after months of not seeing each other, Libby explaining how the jobs weren't for her, she had so much more to give. My words, I thought, but I didn't say anything. Suzy was agreeing with her, saying that life was far too short and she must find something that made her happy. I hadn't told Suzy about the men in Libby's life, just like I hadn't mentioned it since to Libby. I knew she would talk to me about it if she wanted to.

We arrived at the restaurant. As always it was busy. A cheery man showed us to our table. It was a popular place to eat and was full of families, couples, friends. We laughed our way through our meal. Libby had ordered a bottle of wine, as I thought she would. Suzy filled Libby in on her life, admitting she was pregnant, but we weren't to talk about the father. Libby accepted that; I knew she would. I'd have asked so many questions, wanted to know why he wasn't important. Not Libby. It wasn't that she didn't care, but she accepted that things in life happened.

As Suzy told her story, I glared at her, shaking my head discreetly. She nodded the acknowledgement that Libby didn't know about my problem. Libby had assumed I wasn't drinking because I was driving; I went along with that explanation. It was fun to be with them both, forgetting that I had this baggage weighing me down. Libby told some stories about her housemates.

Suzy and I unprofessionally shared some stories about our worst customers. It was good to release some endorphins, to feel washed out from laughing rather than anxiety.

As we were finishing our drinks, I could see Suzy looking at something near the door. Her sparkle diminished and a look of torment crept over her flawless skin.

'What's wrong?' I rubbed her arm. 'Are you okay?'

'Jesus, Suzy, you look like you've seen a ghost.'

'It's him.'

'Who?' Libby asked, craning her neck to see what the fuss was about. 'Oh my God, it's Steve Donnelly.'

'Who?' Suzy looked confused.

'Oh, Kat darling, you are looking well tonight!' A high-pitched squeal belted across the restaurant.

'Oh, hi, Mrs Donnelly.' My practised, professional tone was automatic.

'I tell you what, this girl had me worried, nearly passing out on me, looking like death. Anyone would think she was pregnant!'

People were now staring. I forced myself to smile. A silence fell, as Mrs D looked at me intensely and said, 'You're not, are you?'

'No!'

'You are!'

'I'm not.' I attempted a slight laugh. This was awful. I couldn't possibly allow her to know. It would be all over Facebook and Twitter; emailed, text messaged and telephoned across the country. People who didn't know me would know my business.

'You had me worried there!' she cried. 'I can't have you going off on maternity leave! It would be like losing my cleaner.' She turned to her husband, who was looking round the restaurant, not showing any interest in who we were. 'Stevie darling, this is my beauty therapist and ...' She waited for me to introduce Suzy and Libby, which I did. Libby gave her most charming smile. Suzy twisted her mouth, which wasn't really a smile, more an awkward grimace. Steve nodded at us all confidently, but Suzy didn't look up. She poured herself a glass of wine, rudely ignoring Mrs D and

Steve. I was surprised she wasn't trying to promote her business to them. She would do wonders with Mrs D.

At last, they left us in peace. Suzy finished the bottle of wine, which surprised both me and Libby. She'd said during the meal that she wouldn't be drinking at all for nine months. Here she was, downing a glass of Pinot as if it was water.

'I'm going to make a move,' she said, grabbing at her coat, which was hanging from the back of her seat.

I placed my hand on hers. 'What the hell is wrong, Suzy?'

'That's him.'

'Who?'

'That's Michael.'

'No that's …' It dawned on me. 'Oh, shit.'

'Yeah, oh shit.' Suzy looked over at him. 'I didn't realise he was a footballer. How stupid does that make me?'

'Oh, no! You didn't realise who he was?' Libby caught up.

'No, I didn't. I've been having an affair with Steve Donnelly, but I thought his name was Michael, and that he was an investment guru.'

'You didn't know who *Steve Donnelly* was?'

'No. I don't watch the bloody football, do I?'

'But you're a fitness instructor. I'd thought you'd know things like that.'

'Libby, leave it,' I told her sternly. She was more concerned with who he was than the fact that he was married and had been lying to Suzy; and his wife. He'd admitted he was married, but not who he was. How strange. No wonder he wanted nothing to do with her and the baby. Imagine that all over the headlines! The worst thing was, he hadn't batted an eyelid when he noticed Suzy. He'd not looked uncomfortable at all. He was obviously a pro at this.

How many other times? How many other women? Oh God, poor Suzy.

'Right, come on, let's get the bill and get out of here.' I lifted my hand to the waiter.

'No, you two stay. I'm going to get some air.'

'No. I can't sit here looking at *him*.'

'Can't I finish my drink?'

'Libby, come on.' I glared at her.

Suzy was gone, swiftly making her exit. Libby stood up reluctantly but not before downing the rest of her wine. I quickly paid, handing the young waiter my card, trying to make no eye contact with Mrs D. Pay and leave. Fast as possible. But then, Libby tripped. She staggered across the restaurant, knocking a lady on the head with her handbag. The lady, who'd been enjoying soup, now had it dripping from her nose.

My heart sank like a bag of stones. The whole restaurant was looking at Libby. An elderly woman jumped from her seat, grabbed Libby under her armpits and clumsily tried to lift her, her face turning red with effort. Oh dear Lord, was she going to have a heart attack? But her husband came to the rescue and got Libby back onto her feet. Her usual sleek, dark bob was messed up and she looked as if she'd been dragged through a hedge. I grabbed her arm and headed for the door, after thanking the Samaritan couple and apologising to the staff.

But I wasn't quick enough; Mrs D skipped towards us, hands held high, her 'Oh, my God' voice, high-pitched and annoying, making everyone turn and look at us. She hugged Libby, although she'd never met her before, drawing more attention to us both and herself, then reluctantly she let us leave as we both insisted Libby was fine. I had no idea whether she *was* fine, but I needed to be out of there. I could sort her broken bones out later.

As Mrs D walked back to her table I could see her husband, Steve or Michael (what other names did he use?), staring at us. Did he feel any regret or sadness? Was he wondering where Suzy was? Was he still interested? I wanted to march up to him and tell him to stay away.

Libby was laughing when we got outside, as we updated Suzy on what had happened. Suzy looked tired. Vulnerable and abandoned. I wanted to make it right for her. It was bad enough when she'd found out he was married, but to realise his whole life was a lie must have been another shock. How many personalities did he have tucked away in a secret box? Different stories for different women? Suzy could do so much better.

I told her this, she smiled and looked out the window. She was hurting. I could see that. As I drove, I glanced at her and saw the tear which ran off the end of her nose. She tried to catch it with her sleeve. I patted her leg, without saying a word because I wasn't sure she could speak, or wanted to speak. I didn't think she needed advice or questions of any kind.

'I'm the better person and he's given me the best gift.' She put her hand on her stomach. Her words weren't directed at us. I didn't think she even wanted an answer. So we drove home in silence, our thoughts our own. Our friendship was strong. Our sisterly love was tough.

We dropped her at home, watching her enter her house before driving away. As we pulled out of her road, Libby asked me if I was pregnant.

'What makes you ask that?'

'The look on your face when that awful woman asked you; or accused you, I should say. What's her name?'

'Mrs D. I mean, Donnelly.'

'Does she not have a first name?'

'Yes, but we're not allowed to use it.'

'Silly bitch.' Libby's blunt answer made me smile. 'So, are you?'

'I am, but it's a long story, a secret story, so you can't tell anyone. Especially not Marianne or Dad.'

'But you're not happy?'

'Not really, but I'm sure it'll all be fine.'

'Are you thinking of getting rid of it?' Only Libby could get away with asking such a question and in the manner that she had.

'I'm not sure what to do.'

'What does Max think?' Her phone rang before I had the chance to answer.

I was pleased of the distraction. I didn't want to talk about Max, I had yet to find out what he really thought.

'Strange, it's Marianne.'

I could only hear one side of the conversation, but I knew something serious had happened. I tried to listen while concentrating on the road, straining my ears to hear Marianne's part of the conversation.

Libby hung up and looked at me, tears forming as she shook her head.

'What?' I demanded. 'What's happened?'

'Dad's taken an overdose. He's in hospital.'

18

They allowed two of us into ICU. Nurses spoke quietly as machines beeped and visitors mumbled softly to their loved ones. Following the strict instructions, Libby and I cleaned our hands with the surgical gel which hung beside the entrance.

Dad lay helplessly. Tubes came from his nose, his mouth, his hands and from the blanket that covered him. He looked more peaceful than we'd seen him in years. Even when he was flaked out on the sofa in a comatose state of drunkenness, he didn't look peaceful. His grey, tired face looked old. His thin skin stretched gauntly over his brittle bones. Frail, defenceless and weak, not the sometimes arrogant and often opinionated man we'd become used to. I half expected him to jump up, detach himself from the machines and shout, 'Only joking!' I wished he would.

We sat on the two chairs placed to the right of his bed, listening to the machines beeping in their own rhythm. I studied the serenity on his face, I could see the resemblance from the dad I remembered. I reached out to touch his hand. His long, narrow fingers felt cold and limp. I let it go, not liking the texture of the unresponsive skin. It was strange to touch him, and for him not to feel our presence. It was odd to watch him breathing so peacefully, so contentedly within this unfamiliar environment. It was strange to see him relaxed.

'You can talk to him.' The nurse appeared at the other side of his bed, looked at the machines and made a few notes. Her voice was gentle, soft and soothing. We smiled, unsure of what to say. Embarrassed; Dad wasn't the approachable type. We had to plan what to talk to him about before we engaged in conversation with him. Now, here he was, lying in front of us, and we could say all that we liked, without being subjected to his opinion; and we couldn't speak. We didn't know what to say to him. We found ourselves talking to each other, quietly, almost in whispers. But as we talked we didn't take our eyes off him.

We sat for fifteen minutes before leaving Dad to his dreams. Marianne had kindly let us see him first, probably wanting us to give her the details before she dared go in herself. I sat with Libby in the cold waiting room to ensure Marianne was okay. The wall displayed posters on unprotected sex, heart disease and smoking cessation. It wasn't the happiest of places. Its leaded window was protected by white Venetian blinds that were stained from years of hanging in the same place. The floor was covered with blue carpet tiles and three high-backed brown chairs had been placed strategically. Libby read through an old version of *Now* magazine, while I sat there asking random questions about the celebrities on the front. Not that I was interested; but simple, irrelevant thoughts helped to keep reality at bay. Distraction was my best talent. I'd become a pro since Mum died. It worked well in the salon too. Keeping busy and asking others about their lives helped to pull a blanket of disguise over my own.

Marianne came out half an hour later. She was pale and there were shadows under her frail, ageing eyes; deep lines embedded after years of living with our father. She had obviously sobbed as she spoke to Dad. I wondered what she'd said. Libby hugged her and I followed suit, because it was the right thing to do.

A doctor entered the small stuffy room, as if he'd been waiting for Marianne to join us. I wondered if he'd assumed that Marianne was our mum and I stopped myself from correcting him. His tired face looked formal but warm. At a guess, he was early fifties. Tall, grey and probably quite handsome in his younger days, but now lines had been carved around his eyes, which seemed to tell a harrowing story. I always thought that many men grew better-looking with age, but I wasn't sure he was one of them. He explained that the gastric lavage had gone as well as could be expected (I wasn't quite sure what he was talking about, until Marianne explained once he'd left; Dad's stomach had been pumped). Dad was stable, but still unconscious. He would stay in ICU overnight but they planned to move him to a ward in the morning.

When he left us alone Marianne explained what had happened; how he'd said he was going for a bath and had never came back down. He'd been in the bath an hour, when she realised how much time had passed and she'd shouted up to him. He'd locked the door, she couldn't get to him, she'd banged, she'd shouted, she'd even tried to run at the door with the base of a heavy lamp, to no avail. An ambulance was called. It was the paramedic who'd released him from the bathroom by removing the door handle. Marianne was embarrassed she hadn't thought of that. I told her we all switch off when we're in an intense panic; I knew that feeling too well.

They had lifted his lifeless, naked body onto the stretcher. After finding a pulse they worked hard to keep it going. They believed he'd taken around eighty paracetamol and at least twenty of his diazepam; the empty packets lay there for all to see. There were no other empty boxes or cartons to hint he'd taken anything else. Except the bottle of vodka, which was half-empty and lying next to the tub.

I couldn't help but wonder, why was he naked? If he had every intention of killing himself, why do it naked? What was he thinking? Well, he obviously wasn't. The tears stung but I swallowed them back. I didn't want to cry for him. I didn't want to cry anymore. My emotional imbalance had been stretched too far. I felt like an actress playing in a drama where the world seemed to be moving around me as the main character, the plot moving from strength to strength; but I hadn't read the script. I didn't know my lines. I wasn't sure how I was meant to behave. It didn't feel real.

What if Dad died? I would be sad. It would be traumatic to lose him. But I knew in my heart that we'd already lost him sixteen years ago. He could die without a chance to reconcile our relationship. But what relationship did we have? What was this world he'd created? He was supposed to be responsible for us, but he'd passed the load to another. He was supposed to be our rock, but he was more like a corroded piece of wood, being washed away by the tide of life. He wanted this to end. He didn't want to live.

How would he feel when he realised he'd survived? Would he be angry? Could he actually get any angrier? My poor Dad. I felt sad for him, for this situation, for the life he wanted to leave behind. Maybe after all these years he'd decided it was best to join Mum. What would Mum think? Would she still love the man he'd turned into? If he did succeed, if he didn't wake in the morning, it would end, unfinished. The way it had with Mum.

The part of me that still felt like his little girl wanted him to wrap his arms around me, tell me it would be okay. Hold me tight, cuddle me close, protect me.

I missed him. I missed him more than I'd realised. Probably as much as Mum. I had Mum's spirit around me; I had Dad's shell.

We followed the advice from the nurses and left Dad alone. There was an overnight room but it was uncomfortable so we decided it would be best to come back tomorrow. I knew Marianne would be here first thing. I'd encouraged her to bring Libby with her. I could come back the following evening, my own problems pushed to the back of my mind. I was hoping Max would understand.

We walked away, presenting an image of a distraught family, a closely connected family. I shuddered at the thought of this image. The nurses had treated us as such, even calling Marianne our mum: 'Your mum needs some rest.' Libby had glared at me, silently warning me not to say anything. For once she was the mature one. I'd bit my tongue, wanting to say, 'My mum has been resting for sixteen years, thank you.' But I hadn't said anything, I hadn't corrected them. It felt wrong to embarrass them, make Marianne feel uncomfortable and belittle myself with what would have looked like childish behaviour.

It was the early hours of the morning by the time I climbed under the cool covers, needing to sleep before my customers bombarded me with their own issues. Issues that seemed so irrelevant. I needed to sleep to give me the strength not to air my real opinion of their petty woes.

As I lay my head upon my soft pillow, I felt the lump burst in my throat and I screamed inside as I wept silently. The tears poured from me as I released the emotional blockage which I'd allowed to build up. I cried for Dad. For Mum. For Marianne. For Libby. For Max. For Suzy.

For me.

I cried as I thought about how much I loved Max, but how I didn't want to face him. It shamed me and it hurt me to admit it, as I'd never wanted to avoid him before. Over the last six months I'd never had to ask for his support. I knew it would always be there. I'd always imagined being with someone I could turn to, run to, in times of turmoil. But now all I wanted was space. Space to think about the family we didn't want. I needed to think about Dad and why we were here in this God-awful situation.

I spoke into the darkness, believing Mum could hear me.

'Is this it, Mum? Is this what it comes to? Is this how it ends?'

19

'Max, I need you to understand.' I could hear the desperation in my own voice. I was hoping he could too.

'I do understand, but this problem isn't going to go away.'

'So you agree it's a problem.'

'Don't play those games, Kat, you know what I'm saying.'

'Look, please let me visit Dad tonight. I promise you we'll talk tomorrow.'

Finally, he agreed. I'd have thought he would have been more understanding. I'm not saying he wasn't, but he was desperate to come over after I'd visited Dad. But I didn't know what time it would be. I didn't want to fix a time and then let him down again. I thought that evening I would have a better understanding of what was happening with Dad, giving me more peace of mind to talk with Max the night after.

Marianne had picked up Libby. I'd phoned Suzy, who was devastated. She knew my history, Dad's history: she'd lived through it with us.

'Do you think it's because of today?'

'I think it's exactly that.' If I was honest, I knew that if he was going to do it, it would be around her birthday or the anniversary of her death. I knew this. Maybe other years I'd watched or listened for signs, but the last time I saw him he was fine. When we'd had Marianne's dinner, he'd been fine. Well, as fine as he could be. He'd eaten with us, he'd acknowledged us; he didn't laugh or smile much, but he never did. He must have known what he was going to do. He must have planned it. I don't believe he decided at that moment or that day. I think he wanted it to end before he reached her birthday.

I quietly worked my way through my morning ladies. After I'd told Melanie what had happened, we'd decided to ask Mandy to come in later that afternoon. Mrs D was in straight after lunch and then I had a few ladies who could be passed over to Melanie. It meant I could go to the hospital sooner and if possible maybe see Max afterwards. But I didn't want to build his hopes up, so kept that to myself. The way my world was working at the moment, anything could go wrong.

Libby had arrived back just before lunch. She explained that Dad had been moved to a ward. He was sleeping when they'd visited so they hadn't stayed long. Marianne had left her alone with him, but Libby found it too creepy as at one stage she thought he'd died. When she told me this, her voice almost broke. This surprised me, as Libby had never really expressed her emotions towards Dad, and I remembered the tears she'd pushed away when Marianne had told us how it had happened. It was strange because Libby couldn't remember him any differently from the man he had become. I suppose we were both mourning completely different men.

I told her to go and make us some lunch and I'd join her when I'd finished with my client.

But it was Clare who would change those plans.

'I think we need to talk,' she said solemnly as she entered the salon.

20

'Maxwell doesn't know I'm here.' Her tones were soft. 'Please promise me you won't tell him. He'd be very upset.'

'Promise.' I was pleased he didn't know. When she'd walked through the door, I was about to call him and shout the odds about having his mother fight his battles for him: 'Are you a man or a mouse?' I felt sick that he was getting her involved. I envisaged a future battling against them both. But as we sat in the coffee shop, where I'd taken her to escape prying eyes in the salon, she explained that he hadn't asked her to come. I still felt annoyed, though, that she was here.

'Look, Kathryn, I know things have been difficult but I'm not sure this is the answer.'

'What has he told you?'

'Not much. I'd called him this morning as I haven't seen him for a couple of days. I thought it was very strange that he was ignoring me. He was very upset when I spoke with him.' She waited for a response, but I wasn't going to help her out. I felt she was violating my space. 'He said that you were pregnant and he didn't think you were going to keep it, but you wouldn't talk to him. He also told me under no circumstances to get involved.' She smiled sheepishly.

'Did he tell you my dad is in hospital?' My voice was hard. I sounded as if I was blaming her, but I was incensed that Max would tell her I wouldn't talk to him.

'He did mention it. I'm sorry.' Her voice was kind, which surprised me. I expected her to make sarcastic comments about his inability to be sober, but she looked sad. 'Look, Kathryn, I haven't come here to argue with you, I haven't come to tell you what you should be doing, I wanted to talk to you and tell you I understand.'

I didn't say anything. How could she possibly understand? Clare with her pampered life, her inability to look outside her own box, what would she understand about me?

'When I fell pregnant with Maxwell, I was devastated. I didn't want children.'

'*Really?*' I was shocked. These were words I didn't expect to hear from her.

'He doesn't know this story, so this is completely between us.'

She was reaching out to me. I had to accept it. I had nothing to lose. I could sit and fight her but what would that achieve? I'd wanted her to connect with me and here she was, offering me a part of her. She was trusting me. I wasn't sure I could have asked for much more.

'I promise, it's between us.' Against the background hum of staff serving lunch, machines beeping behind the counter and customers talking amongst themselves, I felt as if Clare and I had stepped over an invisible line.

'Henry worked away a lot when we were younger. I would travel around the world with him. We had a fantastic life. I'd qualified as a hairdresser, but because we did so much travelling I knew I couldn't settle in a job anywhere. We'd decided we would travel for a few years, then we would settle so I could set up my own salon.'

'I didn't realise you were a hairdresser.'

'Well, it didn't happen.'

'Max?'

'I love him with all my heart. You mustn't get me wrong with this, Kathryn. I don't regret any of it and that's why I thought it best you hear my story. I want you to understand that it doesn't have to be the end of the world.'

'But I don't think I can cope with a baby.'

'Neither did I.' She looked at me, her eyes full of kindness I'd never seen from her before. Her hard exterior had vanished.

Gina's words came back to me: 'Deep down she really does have a heart of gold, once you break through that hard shell.' Perhaps she was right.

'I cried for the whole pregnancy. I was married and we had plenty of money. Henry would have left me if I'd decided not to go ahead with the pregnancy. When Maxwell was born I couldn't look at him. I suffered with very bad post-natal depression, although they called it the baby blues in my day. My baby blues went on for most of his first year. He doesn't know this. You mustn't tell him. I feel guilty to this day about the feelings I had towards him.'

'I won't say a word.'

'I never set up my own salon. In fact, I never cut another hair again. Henry continued to work away, I had no support. Henry's mum and dad lived away from us, and my mum was really ill. I was trying to look after my baby and make sure my mum was okay. Anyway, when Maxwell was about nine months old my mum died of cancer.'

She didn't say what type of cancer. It felt inappropriate to ask. She sipped on her cappuccino as if remembering the pain she'd felt.

I didn't know what to say. Saying 'sorry' seemed feeble; it had happened thirty-three years ago, I could sense the pain she obviously still felt. I thought about the pain I felt for my own mum. I'd always put it down to my age: being so young when Mum died was why it was so painful. But for the first time I realised it's the loss of such an important figure, and age doesn't matter.

'Once Mum died I put everything into Maxwell. He was my focus. I realised I'd missed nearly a year of his life and I didn't want to miss anymore. He helped me cope with my mum dying.'

'But don't you think about what life could have been?'

'Of course; who doesn't? But I wouldn't change Maxwell for the world. I wished I'd pursued my own career, I could have done that, but I didn't have anyone to push me or help me. As I said, Henry was away. It seemed such a hassle. I was worried Maxwell would miss out in some way if I had a career, so I left it. We didn't need the money. So I decided to embrace my life as a mother and a wife.'

'Is that why you don't like me? Because I have a salon?' It sounded pathetic when the words came out, but I meant it.

'I like you.' She looked shocked. I looked at her and smiled; we both knew what I was getting at. She blushed as she looked at her cup, as if it would tell her what to say next. She then looked directly at me and smiled genuinely. 'I've not been fair, I know. I'm sorry.'

'It's okay.'

'No. It's not. I've been rude to you and you didn't deserve it. But it wasn't you personally. Admittedly, when I saw your salon, I was a little jealous. I thought about what I could have had. You were bubbly and fun and I can see your salon is your life.'

'That's what worries me: my salon *is* my life.'

'But you can have both.'

'Do you think?'

'Plenty of women do. Plus, you have my support.'

'I'm scared. I'm worried this baby will ruin my life. Max and I haven't been together that long, and my salon is starting to expand.'

'Kat, I really think you need to stop analysing everything so much.' That wasn't the answer I wanted. That wasn't going to tell me whether I was capable of being a mum, or whether I even wanted to be one. 'You're going over it all in your head, but you're in a panic. There's no need to panic.'

'But your career stopped when you had Max.'

'My career hadn't started, that's the difference. You're already there. You don't need to start again, you have a thriving business that will continue to thrive if you want it to.'

'I can't see how having a baby is a good thing. I know that sounds selfish and cruel.'

'It does to anyone who doesn't understand, but I felt the same and honestly there are not many negatives.'

'What about dirty nappies and sleepless nights?' I jested. She knew I was joking; at least, I hope she did. We were talking about the deeper emotions, the parts of a woman that change once she has given birth.

'I think all you've done is think negative thoughts about having a child. The love you will feel for your child will outweigh those feelings.' Her eyes were soft as she took my hands securely within her own. 'You'd make a great mum, Kathryn.'

'I'm scared.' My eyes pricked with tears. I was surprised to feel so connected with the woman I'd hated. She'd opened up to me in a way I never thought possible.

'Most mums are scared.'

'But I've already been through so much. I'm not sure I want to go back to bringing up another child. I gave up so much of my childhood. Do I really want to give up my adulthood too?'

'Libby?' she asked.

I realised how little she knew of my life. I explained briefly about Marianne, and Dad's depression. She nodded knowingly. I explained I'd taken Libby with me when I'd moved out and how I'd always felt responsible for her.

'I don't think it's about giving up your adulthood, Kathryn. I know it must have been so hard for you to bring Libby up. Your mum would be so proud.' She held my hands in hers, and my tears threatened again.

'I think it's about embracing it. This could be your chance to be truly happy.'

'I am truly—' I half-laughed, sniffing away the tears. 'I *was* truly happy.'

'Okay, but let's look at this another way. Would having a termination make you happy?'

As she said the words, I realised I hadn't thought of it that way. I'd simply wanted to return my life back to the way it was, without the complications. But would I be happy if I decided not to have the baby? Would my life return to normal, or would this follow me around forever?

'You've got to think how much you may regret this. Yes, you might have been quite happy not having children, but the opportunity is here now. I truly believe you could make this work. You could make this baby fit in with your life instead of the other way around.'

'Do you think?'

'I think you will regret it if you let this baby go.'

'What if I die, Clare?' The lump formed once again, sticking in my throat, choking my words.

Clare gripped my hands tighter. Love and compassion shone from her face. 'Kathryn, I totally understand why you feel so scared, but what happened to your mum is not the usual occurrence. You can't live in fear.'

'But it was so hard without her.'

'I understand that, but you're holding onto something that doesn't have to affect you any more. You and Maxwell could have a family of your own. You could show that child all the things you wished you could have participated in when you were growing up. You need to think what this could do for your life.'

'Thank you, Clare.' I meant it. I really wanted her to understand how much I appreciated her making this effort.

'You're more than welcome. I'm sorry I've been so hard on you.'

'That's okay.' I smiled.

'Plus, I didn't want to mention this, but I think it's important.'

'What?'

'Gina.' My heart sank and she must have seen my shoulders droop. I freed my hands from her grip, picking up my drink. 'There is nothing to worry about with Gina.'

'Did Max tell you that?'

'He did, but that doesn't matter. I know he loves you. He never spoke about Gina in the way he talks about you. I was jealous. You were this new, wonderful woman in his life, owning the salon I wanted to own. I thought you were going to take him away from me.'

'I'd never tried—'

'I know, but hopefully one day you'll understand.' She smiled. 'Paula and I are very good friends. Because of that I saw Max and Gina frequently, as we always did things with both families. I'm sorry I was so hostile with you. I was so focused on keeping Max close, I think I lost it for a while. Henry wasn't happy with me. He thinks a lot of you. He says you remind him of me.'

'Really?' I smiled.

If she'd said that yesterday I'd have probably enrolled on a course on how to become a better person or change your personality. But as we sat opposite each other, our lives intertwined, two women with their own problems and sufferings, I felt proud to be connected to Clare. I would be proud to be like her. For once, I felt no guilt as I thought of my own mum.

I felt as if Clare had been brought into my life for a reason.

I knew what I had to do.

21

Back in the salon, peacefulness surrounded me. The unsettled waters that had been washing over me were calm. I knew everything would be okay. I'd wanted to ask Clare about the hillbillies comment but had left it, as I didn't want to ruin this new-found friendship.

I had Mrs D's appointment, then Mandy would be taking over for the afternoon. I planned to go and see Dad and then, definitely, see Max. The desire to avoid him was replaced by an urge to embrace him. I wanted to hear how he really felt about this baby. I wanted to listen to him. I was amazed that it was Clare who had lifted the fog that had been clouding my mind.

Clare, with her own secrets. I wondered if Gina knew her story.

'Morning, Mrs Donnelly.' My professional smile switched on automatically.

She nodded, her big, dark sunglasses covering her eyes.

'Do you want to follow me?' I asked. She nodded again. I was perturbed. I wondered if she was avoiding someone or if she expected the paparazzi to be waiting for her. 'We're in room one, Mel.'

'Okay.' Melanie frowned, looking puzzled by Mrs D's subdued behaviour.

Mrs D followed me, her head down as we entered the small, scented room where lavender soothed our senses. Soft spa music played in the background, the aromatic candles flickered gently across the pale pink walls and the low lighting was perfect for the facial and massage Mrs D was about to embark on. Her whole body was refreshed every week as I worked on the knots that she thought she had. I don't think I'd ever discovered one tense muscle in her body.

'Would you like to make yourself—'

'Oh Kat, it's awful!' She broke down, collapsing into the cushioned chair, and let out a heartfelt sob. She leaned forward, her head in her hands, her peroxide white hair falling forward, unusually unkempt and messy. I leant down by her side, resting my hand on her knee where her skinny jeans clung tightly to her slim thighs, and asked if she was okay. Stupid question, really. It was obvious she wasn't.

'I found out last week he's been sleeping with my so-called best friend and then this morning I received a letter from some woman who says she's having his baby.' She lifted her head up. Mascara had run down her thin cheeks. The confident young woman looked like a lost little girl. Her high cheekbones, which were normally decorated with wisps of bronzer, were pale. Her permanent lip make-up was etched impeccably, but the gloss which would typically accompany the outline was non-existent, leaving a plumped, dry mouth, which looked sore and uncomfortable.

'Oh God, I'm sorry.' I swallowed. Surely it wasn't Suzy who had sent the letter? I handed Mrs D some tissues, feeling useless and wishing she wasn't confiding in me.

'I asked Diane if she'd written the letter,' she told me. I assumed Diane must have been the so-called best friend. 'She denied it and then she had the cheek to tell me to look at the type of man I was married to. She had the cheek to give me advice.'

'Oh Mrs Donnelly, I am sorry.'

'Oh, call me Ange.' She took a deep breath and sat back in the chair. 'They've been at it for months.' She blew her nose into a tissue. 'I've hardly slept all week. She only came round for a glass of wine and then bombarded me with it.'

'She *told* you?'

'Yeah.' A teary smile trembled round her lips. 'She thought it best I know, because she wasn't the only one, apparently. She got that right.'

'Oh.' I didn't know what to say. I had to be cautious about speaking my thoughts to customers: they came to us to sound off and feel better, but more often than not they didn't want our opinion. They didn't want to be judged. They just wanted to be listened to.

'Yeah, apparently he's at it all over the place, my friends, at the gym, on nights out.' She started to cry again. 'I thought he loved me.'

'I'm sure he does, in his own way.' Stupid, I know, but as I said, I didn't know what to say. If it had been Libby or Suzy, I'd have been shouting the odds. Leave the bastard! I couldn't say that to Mrs D, or Ange, as she'd now downgraded herself.

'That's what he said.' She laughed bitterly. 'When Di had left last week, he begged me. He said she was lying, it was a one-off, she'd wanted more but he loved *me*. She was making it all up. I really wanted to believe him. I really wanted to make it work. I love him.'

'Well, maybe she *did* write the letter herself.' I knew she hadn't but I was trying to make Mrs D feel better.

'I don't think so.' She shook her head. 'I don't understand it: Steve and I are always at it. He shouldn't have the energy to go anywhere else.'

I stroked her leg. I was scared that if I opened my mouth I would tell her about Suzy. That would make me the worst person ever. I wanted to tell her I knew he was a prick and she could do so much better than him. But I couldn't do that. Not without having to explain how I knew.

She sat for an hour, crying, sobbing into my shoulder, telling me tales about her marriage. Telling me how she couldn't possibly be with someone else. She didn't know how to move on. Steve was her world. She'd been with him fifteen years; they'd been at school together. I knew all of this. Childhood sweethearts, she'd say proudly in the salon, aiming this at anyone who wanted to take any notice of her. She told me how for her thirtieth birthday (which was in the coming weeks) he'd organised a huge cocktail party. How he'd always surprised her with many gifts. How he always made her feel special.

I thought back to what Suzy had said about Michael (aka Steve), how he'd showered *her* with gifts and made *her* feel special.

Mrs D also told me how they'd been trying for a baby and it wasn't happening. She asked me if I thought that's what he was doing: trying for a child with someone else.

I shook my head and nearly said, *I can assure you that's not the case*, then remembered where I was and pulled my thoughts back on track. For a fleeting moment I thought she might be tricking me and that she knew about Suzy. I felt nausea rising. I'd been doing pretty well with the whole sickness thing of late (well, today) but the thought that perhaps she knew what I knew sent the sickness flooding over me like a wave pool. But she didn't, I was sure of it. She was intent on telling her story and getting all her emotions out. She just needed to express and not be judged. I didn't think she wanted my advice, as she could have got that from her friends; although she said she wasn't sure who to trust. Don't trust *me*, I wanted to say, feeling desperately uncomfortable.

She insisted on paying me for the hour. I shook my head vigorously as she stood with her debit card in her hand. I refused to let the machine accept her card.

She laughed and said, 'Let's take him for all he's got.'

I wanted to do that more than Mrs D could ever imagine, so I accepted her offer, resisting the urge to type in £4,000 rather than £40.

She seemed pleased I was being so kind, and not judging her. Then she left, her face no more sorted out than it had been when she'd arrived. It was probably the only time she really needed the treatments.

'I'm here anytime,' I said as she was leaving; but I didn't really mean it, as I'd found the whole hour torture. She didn't reply, but folded some notes and placed them in the pocket of my black tunic and shook her head firmly when I protested.

I felt guilty. I felt as if I was betraying her. I didn't deserve her gratitude.

I need to speak to Suzy; had it been her who'd sent the letter?

22

I left the salon once Mandy had arrived to help. Libby had ventured out after I'd totally forgotten I'd sent her up to the flat to make lunch. I had no idea where she'd gone. Normally I would have grilled her, warning her to stay away from Howard, Alan or whoever else was causing drama in her life. But I didn't care at that moment. She was an adult. I had my own problems.

I'd tried to ring Suzy but there was no answer. I knew she might be out training, but I decided I would call at her house on the way to the hospital. I needed to settle my mind. I needed to make sure she was okay. If she had sent the letter, what was she thinking? It was totally out of character.

As I pulled into her road, I saw the Range Rover Sport parked on a grass verge, a random spot that was partly blocking a driveway. I quickly pulled into a space and jumped from my car. Suzy's front door was ajar and panic set in as I ran across the grass to her home. I heard something smash as I pushed open the door, my heart racing.

'You fucking bitch!' I heard him roar.

The coffee table had been overturned in the living room and a vase had been smashed. I entered the kitchen at full force. One of Steve's hands was around her neck, holding her against the wall. In the other was a knife.

'Let her go!' I screamed. My heart was beating painfully fast as I stared at the shiny sharp blade that was inches from her face.

'I'm going to fucking kill her! And you'll be next if you don't fuck off.'

Suzy couldn't speak. Her face was puce and blood dripped down one side of it. He was holding her off the floor by her throat.

My instinct was to run at him. I looked around for something I could hit him with, but there was nothing. He wouldn't need the knife if I didn't do something quick. Talk to him! Talk! I could hear my breath rattling as I tried to stay calm.

'Look, Steve.' My voice was shaking. 'This is not a good idea. If you do anything stupid, you'll be locked up for a very long time.'

'It won't matter, cos this *bitch*,' he spat the words at Suzy, 'has ruined my life anyway.'

'Now come on, let's look at the bigger picture here. You will get life in prison, forget your football, forget your wife, forget your life as you know it.'

He didn't answer me.

I wondered if I'd hit a nerve. Keep going, I told myself, desperate for him to let her go. 'Ange isn't going to want you in prison is she? You guys could still make a go of this.' I hoped by using her first name I'd connect with him.

'She deserves to fucking die.'

'Come on.' I took a step forward, slowly, not having any clear plan. Grab him? Grab the knife? Jump on him? I didn't know! 'Suzy made a mistake. She won't ever bother you again.'

'She'll be having my kid then asking for child maintenance and all that crap. Money-grabbing whore, like all the rest of you.'

'She won't.'

Suzy's eyes were starting to shut. I felt fear completely taking over my body as I ran towards him. I pushed him sideways, but he lurched towards her with the knife, missing her by centimetres. It forced him to let her go and she slumped to the floor.

'Bitch!' he screamed at me.

I backed away, tripping over a toppled chair. My backside hit the floor, sending a shooting pain up my back. My baby! He leaned over the chair towards me, pure hatred filling his eyes as the knife pointed directly at me.

'Please, think of your life,' I begged him weakly. 'You don't want to go to prison, you have too much to lose.'

He stood up, walked towards Suzy, bent down and grabbed her face. 'You stay away from me and my family, or I swear I will hunt you down and rip every limb from your fucking body.' He pushed her head away. It banged against the cupboard. As he stood, he swung back his thick leg and kicked her forcefully in the stomach. Her squeal of pain echoed throughout the house. My heart ached as I tried to untangle my legs from the chair.

He dropped the knife on the floor, staring at me with burning eyes. 'I will kill her.'

His words pierced a hole through my soul and I knew he was serious. As he left the house, I crawled across the floor to Suzy. Her breathing was low. For a dreadful moment I thought I'd lost her. I wrapped her in my arms and we hugged as she cried. I cried too. Relief, terror, fright: I had no idea. I couldn't believe this was happening. My quiet life was turning into something I'd watched on the television, a soap opera. I'd said it was like a film but I didn't have the script. Well, this part I definitely didn't see coming.

Blood dropped onto my arm. I lifted Suzy's face to see where it was coming from. A cut above her eye looked nasty, an open wound that would definitely need stitching. 'We're going to have to go to the hospital.'

'No!' she cried as she pulled herself into a sitting position, holding her stomach and wincing with pain. 'They'll ask questions.'

'Well, don't you think we should call the police?'

'No, absolutely not!' She breathed deeply, the red marks around her neck livid as she rubbed them with her hands. The usual blonde sleek hair scruffily edged her fragile face.

'Suzy, seriously, you can't let him get away with this.'

'I can, because I know he'll kill me, Kat. I thought I was going to die.' Her body went into convulsions of despair and terror.

'Okay, whatever you think is best,' I told her, bringing her back in for a hug. It sounded as if we were talking about an outfit she might be wearing, or where we might go out to eat. *You choose, whatever you think is best.* The words didn't match the seriousness of what had just happened. I lifted myself from the floor, my back feeling the bruising that was already developing. Wetting a cloth, I placed it above Suzy's eye, telling her we really needed to go to the hospital. She didn't want to go. 'Wrap a scarf around your neck. If you don't get that stitched up you're going to have a nasty scar there.' She didn't seem deterred by this fact. 'You'll be reminded of him every time you look in the mirror.'

She looked at me and gave in. 'Right, okay.' I helped her to her feet. She held her stomach, pain obviously running through her. I rearranged the chairs that had been thrown around the kitchen and made her sit down. I found out later that when he'd chased her, she'd thrown chairs around the table in the hope they'd get in his way, hoping she could escape through the front door, but he'd grabbed her hair. She'd been petrified; she really thought he was going to kill her.

I found her a scarf and we went out to the car. As we drove I wondered what else could possibly go wrong. Things seemed to keep spiralling completely out of control.

'Did you send the letter?' I dared to ask as we drew closer to the hospital.

'I know it was stupid,' she said. I could hear the anger in her voice.

'Why did you do it? I thought you were happy about the baby. You seemed so full of life last night.'

'I know, then when I saw them together again last night and he completely ignored me. Who the fuck does he think is? Coming into my life, turning it upside down.' She took a deep breath. 'I got in last night, drank a few more glasses, wrote the letter, then went and posted it at his house.'

'How?'

'I drove,' she whispered.

'You drove?' I asked, horrified that she could be so stupid.

'I know; please don't lecture me. It was about three this morning.'

'That makes it okay? You must have had nearly a full bottle of wine. Suzy, what on earth were you thinking?'

'I wasn't thinking. I didn't feel that drunk. I was fine. But I felt this overwhelming urge to tell her what a dick her husband was.'

'Oh my God, Suzy.' I couldn't think of anything else to say. My best friend, who didn't believe in drinking on a school night, as we called the nights before work, was now pregnant and drink driving. I couldn't comprehend this. It didn't compute.

'My mum can't find out about any of this. When I tell her about the baby, please don't mention it.'

'Come on, like I would.' I shook my head. 'Let's face it, she wouldn't believe me.'

'I know. Kat, what has happened to me?' Suzy looked desperate, staring at me as if I knew the answers.

'Love, hormones, combination.' I smiled, pulling into the busy hospital car park. 'The weather, who knows? The world is going a bit crazy at the moment.'

My phone rang as I pulled into a space. I quickly snapped it open, hoping it wasn't Melanie and there was some drama at the salon.

'Kat, it's your dad: he's taken a turn for the worse.' Marianne spoke softly as she delivered the news. I wished it had been Melanie with a problem at the salon, something I could control, a problem I could have solved.

There was no solution to helping my dad. But how I wished there was.

23

I helped Suzy register at A&E, but left her alone whilst I ran through the hospital to the ICU. As I made my way through the inside corridors, diverting through outside walkways, I realised how depressed and ill everyone looked, even the visitors. I wasn't quite sure who was a patient, except for the ones in dressing gowns sneaking outside for a crafty cigarette.

An elderly lady was walking along on crutches, her purple slippers swishing across the floor, unable to lift her legs. A man with an unshaven face glared at me as if I'd invaded his home, muttering something under his breath. Nurses talked loudly about a patient, inappropriately discussing his bad habits, including dirtying the bed.

I was surprised to see Libby already there, sitting in the drab, uninspiring room that we'd sat in last night. The smell of disinfectant and sweaty bodies turned my stomach. Libby hugged me, and the smell of her perfume hit me. She'd been crying. Her eyes were red and her cheeks flushed, although instead of making her looked wrecked, as tears did to me, she looked young and vulnerable.

'What are you doing here?' I asked. I didn't mean it to sound so accusing.

'I came back after lunch; you'd disappeared.'

'Long story.' I changed the subject. I was glad she hadn't told me she was coming back as I would have been worried. Libby thinks only of herself, hence the reason I thought she'd gone off with her married man for the afternoon. I felt a twinge of guilt that I'd misjudged her. But then, the afternoon's events had shown me that I possibly didn't know any of my family and friends: Suzy committing moral and illegal offences, plus Clare with her understanding nature.

Marianne explained that Dad had stopped breathing. The doctors had been surprised; they weren't expecting the cardiac arrest as he'd woken up after Marianne and Libby had left him earlier and chatted briefly to the nurses. They couldn't explain what had happened.

But Dad didn't want to be here. I don't mean in the hospital, I mean alive. I wondered if he'd panicked when he woke up and realised he hadn't made it; he'd not done the job properly.

I asked if I could see Dad alone. The others agreed. Entering the room that seemed alive, with all its machines beeping, I felt a surge of loss. He shouldn't be here. I had the urge to dismantle his machines and tell the doctors to let him go. He looked peaceful, but his unshaven appearance, his grey, saggy skin, aged him. The embedded lines, the dark circles, the grey, lifeless hair was just his carcass. His soul was trapped deep inside.

I'd always blamed him. Not for Mum dying, but for his attitude towards her dying. The way he'd handled it, the way he'd coped: or not coped, as the case may be. What could I have done? There must have been *something*. There must have been. It was easy at twelve years old to switch off and blame someone else, it was easy to fall into that way of life. He'd needed us as much as we'd needed him. We'd failed him as much as he'd failed us.

I sat by his side and told him everything. I told him I was pregnant, I told him about Clare. I told him about Suzy. I told him about what was happening in Libby's life. I talked to him as if he could hear everything I said. Every word counted. I wanted him to talk back to me. I wanted him to squeeze my hand and I wanted him to tell me it would be okay. I spoke to him as if he was the dad I remembered from Lampford Hall. The dad who I ran through the water jets with. The dad who I'd wished was still with me.

I felt encircled with comfort; a love that had been missing from my life for far too long.

I held his frail face in my hands, kissed his forehead, whispered gently into his ear and told him for the first time in sixteen years, 'I love you.'

24

Suzy came home with me and Libby. She'd had a few stitches. The doctor advised there would be a scar but it would be minuscule compared to the gaping scar she would have had otherwise. She was a little nervous about going home. To be honest, I didn't want to leave her alone.

We shared my bed, a common occurrence. Many nights we'd been out drinking and would land in either her bed or mine. I listened to her gentle snores, her soft breathing, as the day's events ran through my mind. This much trauma hadn't taken place in the last few years let alone a few days. *It never rains but it pours.* Marianne's words rolled through my head. I found myself thinking about her gentle tendencies. I usually dismissed her. Not to her face, but in my thoughts. I had no room to think about her in my life. As I've said, any kind of time or effort given to Marianne felt like an insult to Mum.

But Mum wouldn't have been proud of my behaviour. Libby had more time for Marianne. She made the effort that I didn't. I always believed it was because Libby wanted something from her; she was too self-centred to think of anyone else. But arriving at the hospital today, I'd felt left out of something. I wasn't sure what, I wasn't even sure I wanted to be part of it. But I thought maybe I'd underestimated Libby, and been unfair. She was my sister. We'd been through the same tragedy together. She was younger than me, and maybe I hadn't offered that motherly support that I thought I had. Had she turned to Marianne and I hadn't realised?

I'd not allowed Marianne into my life. She'd never visited my flat, she'd never visited the salon, she didn't know much about my life. I wasn't rude to her. I was never disrespectful. But I didn't include her. I didn't do it on purpose, as such, but I'd accepted that we would never get along. When I was younger I would have planned it that way, but as I'd developed into an adult I'd allowed it to happen. Watching Libby and Marianne together made me feel sad that I'd blocked something out that I could have been part of.

I had a restless night's sleep, dreaming about being chased by a nursery of babies who were trying to get my own baby away from me. They were all far too small to walk. I didn't know much about babies, but this was freaky. I'd never been one to suffer with nightmares, but all of sudden I was faced with horrendous night sweats.

I checked my phone for the time. 6.47a.m. glared back at me, as did a text from Max.

How r u? R we still on 4 2nite? xxx

Yes, we are, can I come to yours? Libby staying here. xxx

He'd obviously been waiting for my reply because he texted back straight away to say that was fine.

Now I had to get through the day without any traumas. I wasn't sure that was possible. I didn't dare wonder what else could go wrong. I was going to open the doors and windows of the salon and enjoy the warm weather, listen to the customers and survive.

It worked. Finally the day was over and no-one had interrupted me, no phone calls had me rushing away. The only drama was Melanie's but it involved an argument with her mother about a long-lost uncle who'd turned up. She'd announced to our customers, 'We only have two weeks to go and she's wanting me to invite some random fella and his family.'

Suzy had gone home, calling me when she got there. She was safe and there were no signs that Steve had been back. I didn't think he would. I think he had simply lost the plot, in an angry moment that could have cost him his career, his family and his life. Surely he would have realised that now. I still thought Suzy should have gone to the police, but she was adamant that wasn't going to happen.

I arrived at Max's after I'd visited Dad in hospital. They'd kept him in ICU. They weren't happy with his breathing so it was best to be safe. I was looking forward to him waking up. I was going to really make an effort. I felt that this warning was my opportunity for us to start again. If I tried, maybe he would try. If I made the effort maybe he would make the effort. Part of me knew I was dreaming. He wanted the alcohol more, but I blocked that part out. I didn't want to go there. I imagined a life of happiness.

Max let me into his house, the place I'd started to think of as my second home. The place where I could see us making a life together. He didn't kiss me, he just let me walk through to the kitchen.

'Would you like a cup of tea?' he asked politely, as if I was a visitor. Someone who'd come to meet with him about work. I nodded. My sickness had eased considerably and I was dying for a glass of wine, but thought it best not to ask for one.

We sat in the living room, where we normally spent our Saturday nights watching films. The black leather sofa was not a choice of mine but I'd added red fleece throws that matched the décor in the room. Instead of sitting together as we normally would, we sat apart like strangers. Away from each other as if we'd never spent hours in bed together, never touched each other, didn't know the rhythm of each other's heartbeat. It felt strange to have him at such a distance, not so much physically but emotionally.

'Why don't you want it?' Max asked me, as if I was a witness on a stand.

Dare I lie? I didn't think so. 'I'm scared,' I admitted, sounding like a small child.

'Of what?' he asked gently.

'Everything. All of it.'

'But we'll do it together. I'm scared too.'

'Are you?'

'Oh God, yeah. I don't know what we're supposed to do with a baby, but many people manage it.' His warmth made me want him, need him.

'But then there's Gina.' I had Clare's words ringing in my head, but I needed to hear them from Max.

'I've told you, there is no me and Gina. I don't know how to prove it to you. Joe is so happy with her. I haven't seen her, but I assume she's the same. I love you, Kat.'

'I love you too, but we've only been together six months. This would be a huge commitment. It's not as if we can change our minds once the baby is here.'

'But it will be fine.' He came and sat next to me, pulling me close to him, bringing me into his warmth, his arms protecting me. 'So, what do you say?'

'I don't know, Max.' My voice trembled as I spoke. 'There's been so much going on, I haven't really thought properly.' It was a lie: it was all I *had* thought about. Even in the midst of all the other crises, it was always there.

'You're talking about this as if we're deciding where to go on holiday.'

'No, I'm just saying, it's been busy.'

'You're making excuses.'

'No, I'm not. You know what the salon's like and—'

'We've made this baby, this is our responsibility. Look, I didn't want children,' I noted the past tense, 'but we've got to deal with this.'

'There is a way of dealing with it.'

'Kat, I feel like I don't know you. Having an abortion because it doesn't fit in with our lives, it's not right.'

'But we have a choice.'

'I totally agree with you,' he nodded. 'But I don't think we deserve that choice.'

'Everyone deserves the choice,' I snapped at him.

'You don't get it, do you?' I bit my lip. I actually felt anxious; nervous of his stance on this. A peculiar sensation, as Max was my equal and never once had I ever felt intimidated. But the passion behind his conviction was leaving me overwhelmed.

'I get that you want us to really think about this.' I knew I wasn't saying what he wanted to hear.

'No, Kat, I've already thought about it. I want this baby. I can't live with myself or with you if you do this.' He stood up and walked across the room. 'We have no real, concrete reason, except a selfish notion that we want holidays, nice clothes, nice cars and all the materialistic things. It's not a good enough reason. We can afford a baby, we could still live a very nice lifestyle, we wouldn't have to give up that much.'

'It's not about that.'

'Then what is it about? Talk to me.' He sat down on a chair at the other end of the room.

I wanted to open up to him like I had Clare, but I couldn't find the words. 'It's lots of things.' I obviously knew my reasons but I couldn't bring myself to tell him. He ran his hands through his hair, looking tired and worn out. He spoke quietly but deeply, his words barely audible as his distressed eyes looked directly at me, as if searching for my soul. 'I don't want to pressurise you but we can do this.'

'Do you really think we can?'

'I know we can.'

I was panicking inside. A decision needed to be made. Clare's words pierced through me. I think I knew when I'd left her that I wanted to keep the baby. I knew in my heart, but making this decision with Max made it final. Made it real.

Max was staring at me, searching my face. 'So … are you not adamant you want an abortion?' I could hear the hope in his voice.

'I'm so scared.' I told him again.

He came back over to me, kneeling in front of me. I thought he was going to propose, and backed off a little. There was still a distance between us. Could we reconnect and make things right? Put our life back on the track we were comfortable with? Whatever we decided now, our lives would never be the same again. Whatever our decision, it would stay with us forever. Dates would be burned into our minds. Every year that passed would be a reminder of what could have been, and every year we would think about the birthday or the date of termination.

'I'm scared too,' he said. 'We'll do this together.'

'You won't let me down?'

'I promise I won't let you down.'

'Right, then.' I took a deep breath.

'Does that mean we're having a baby?' He practically whispered.

'I think so.' I smiled.

We chatted into the early hours. We discussed how having a baby could increase the pleasure in our lives, how we could enjoy the happiness we heard other parents talking about. I tried not to focus on the sleepless nights, the dirty nappies, the crying or the constant need for attention. Max promised he would help. I voiced my thoughts about my business and how I was scared I couldn't maintain that level of activity. The hectic schedules, the demanding customers, the networking, the promoting, the accounts, the diligence it took to squeeze all of this in. Max assured me that we would work all this out, my business didn't have to suffer. We could hire more staff: perhaps working less hours would do me good.

I'd laughed; my life was already changing and soon it would be altered beyond recognition. I would become someone's mum, I wouldn't be me. I'd lose my identity. I'd heard so many women say it when they'd walked through our door.

Max had to keep calming me down. You'll only lose it if you let it happen, he told me. Every time I went into a panic about the smallest detail, such as how to feed a baby, he'd steadily tell me that there were plenty of professionals we could ask and we couldn't be the only people who didn't have a clue where to start. I'd rushed on about our time being taken up, our lives never being the same again. Max thought we should take one step at a time, embrace this new life, take this opportunity and make it work for us. This was typical Max: Mr Positive Approach to Everything; let's make demanding, squealing, messy babies work for us. I remembered what Clare had said.

Perhaps they were both right. Perhaps we *could* make it work.

I wasn't sure we were making the right decision, but I also wasn't sure having an abortion was the right decision either.

I remembered Mum once saying, 'Do nothing, if you're not sure, then do something when you are.' We were actually talking about me spending my birthday money: did I go for the dress or the shoes? Such inconsequential decisions, but to me this had been vital. I wish this decision was as frivolous. In this case, 'Doing nothing,' meant changing our lives for ever, adding an addition to our lives. Becoming three, instead of two. The thought of this actually happening, us actually having a baby made my stomach churn.

A small wave of uncertainty rushed through me, mixed with a fluttering of nerves. I wondered if I was feeling excitement. No. I couldn't be. I was petrified, anxious; let's face it, absolutely scared stiff!

And I must admit, I was worried about the love I'd feel for my baby. What if that love was taken away?

'But, what if nothing ever happens, which is more than likely, and you could feel that love for ever?' Max had said when I'd explained my fears.

I'd never thought of it like that. I thought how beautiful that would be to love another unconditionally for ever. 'This will be an exciting adventure.' Max kept telling me.

I stayed with him that night. It was good to be with him again, I'd missed him so much. It felt wonderful to feel his touch, his warmth, to feel him inside me. To be submerged in his love, his passion, his need for me, his longing for me.

'Move in with me, Kat,' he said, as my head rested against his chest. I ran my fingers down it, considering what he had said.

'Well, we can't all live in my flat, can we?' I smiled, looking up at him.

Meeting my gaze, he kissed my forehead and told me he loved me.

We fell asleep in each other's arms.

The decision was made.

25

'Did you stay out last night?' Libby asked when I walked back into the flat. She was clearly surprised to see me entering from the outside.

'Glad you noticed,' I sarcastically replied as I poured myself a coffee.

'I went to bed early. I'm shattered. I don't know what's going on with me at the moment but I'm knackered all the time.' She was still dressed in pyjamas, eating toast with chocolate spread. It sickened me because she was only a size ten. It was as if *she* ate it, but *I* gained the weight.

'Well, look at your diet. It's crap! You drink most nights, stuff your face with rubbish all day and wonder why you're shattered.' I stirred my coffee and turned to look at her.

'So, did you stay at Max's?' she asked, deftly changing the subject.

'No, I stayed at the dirty old man's down the road. Of course I stayed at Max's.'

'So are you guys okay?'

'Yes, we are.' I smiled. 'Yeah, we're good.'

'So, does that mean I'm going to be an aunty?' She bit her lip, waiting for my response.

'Yes, it does.' I laughed as she ran to hug me, knocking against me as coffee slopped down the outside of the mug. I placed it on the side and hugged her back.

'You're making the right decision.'

'You think?' I was surprised by her reaction. My laid-back sister, whose world revolved around her, was more ecstatic than me.

'This will be the making of you.' She pulled back and clapped her hands. 'I'm so excited.'

'Great.' I laughed, unsure of how to deal with Libby when she was like this. I thought it best not to mention moving in with Max. We had plenty of time to talk about that. I didn't want her to be homeless, but I also didn't want her thinking it would be okay to stay in the flat rent free. Not because I was being cruel and selfish: quite the opposite. All I wanted was for Libby to sort her life out and living off me wouldn't help her do that. But her enthusiasm for our news, her genuine delight, told me to leave that conversation for another time.

Melanie was already in the salon by the time I was sorted. She looked as if she'd been crying. Her usual cheery face was stony as she sorted out her nail desk.

'Are you okay?'

'Do you know what, Kat? I'm not!' Her voice was shaking with anger. 'It's two weeks tomorrow until my wedding. Two fucking weeks and I have no band, an extra five people to seat, half the guests haven't replied, you'd think it was my mother's wedding and to top it all off, me and Bobby fell out last night.' She started to cry. 'I told him I didn't want to marry him anymore.'

'Oh Mel, come here.' I brought her in for a cuddle.

'It's supposed to be the happiest time of my life, this amazing day, but it's all so shit.'

'Look, it *is* a stressful time. How many times have we heard that in here?'

'I know, I've told myself this.'

'Right, ring Bobby, tell him you're sorry—'

'But it was his fault.'

'I don't care, is it worth all this upset? Don't you want to kiss and make-up?' She nodded. 'Right, go on, go and phone him.'

I searched through the diary making a mental note of the customers who were due in over the next couple of days, while Melanie made the call.

Her face was full of smiles when she came back out. 'Sorry,' she said.

'Don't be silly. Are you guys okay now?'

'Yeah,' she smiled, and sat at her nail desk. 'It's really stressing me out. I can't wait for it to be over. I'm looking forward to my honeymoon, more than I am this wedding.'

'I meant to ask you, do you think Mandy might work? I know we'd blocked you out and given Sophie some treatments, but there are plenty of appointments she could cover.'

'I don't see why not,' Melanie said. 'She likes it here.'

'Well, that's good because we might need her a bit more than we'd originally thought.'

'Why?' Concern crossed her face.

'It's only early days, but I'm pregnant.'

'Oh my God, that's great news.' She started rising from her seat but perhaps I hadn't got my thrilled face right yet, because she stopped and said, 'Isn't it?'

'Yes.' I laughed and nodded. 'I think it is.' We hugged. I felt a flutter of delight; or something that wasn't regret. 'Right, well I've got a few phone calls to make, then we'll get this day started. Would you mind chasing Mandy and asking about your honeymoon?'

'No probs.'

'Please don't mention anything to her about me yet. I haven't spoken to a doctor, or midwife, or whatever it is I'm supposed to do.'

'No probs.' She smiled.

Firstly, I rang Marianne to ask about Dad, but she was getting ready to go and visit him and had no news yet. So I rang the hospital, who told me there was no change. I was relieved that Dad's condition was stable.

Secondly, I rang the doctors, advising of my situation and asking what would be the next step. Now the path had been chosen, I felt I needed to deal with this full on. I couldn't block it out any longer. I'd thought I was about seven or eight weeks but Suzy had read that we would probably be about three or four weeks already when we found out. So I was probably around eleven weeks. When I told her my sickness had eased, she said she thought I was over twelve weeks and then in her kindest way added that my waist did look as if it was expanding.

I explained all this to the receptionist, though I doubt she needed to know it all. She told me I needed to speak to the midwife and she put me on hold for at least a minute. I actually thought she'd hung up on me but then realised the dreadful music was still playing. Finally, a cheery woman called Pam came on the phone. She was a midwife and said that the receptionist had told her my story. *Oh, you don't know my story*, I wanted to say. She'd had a cancellation for the following Monday at 9a.m. She said they were extremely busy, so I would be wise to take the slot.

9a.m. Monday morning. It was Mrs D's usual slot. It started her week, she once told me.

I told the midwife I'd take it, then I rang Mrs D.

Luckily she was happy to change her appointment. Normally she would have made me feel useless: 'Kathryn this isn't good enough now, is it?'

I assumed her emotional outburst had helped to break down her barriers. I felt the need to ask how she was; it would be rude not to.

'We're going to work through things. He's been under a lot of pressure; apparently the baby thing was a scam, some deranged fan. He loves me, Kathryn.' Mrs D was back, Ange was lost inside her.

I felt as if I was betraying her when I told her I was pleased for her. I didn't think she was truly happy. I think she'd lost her identity and she didn't know what to do to get it back. I wanted to shout, 'Move on!' but thought better of it.

Finally, I rang Suzy. I wanted to check she was okay, as I knew Steve and his dramatics had really knocked it out of her. Literally. But I knew she would be pleased with my news. I knew she'd be so excited for me.

'Kat, I think I've got a problem.'

'What?'

'I woke up this morning and I'm bleeding.'

'Lots?'

'Not really, but it's definitely there.'

'Have you phoned a midwife or anything?'

'I phoned the doctors, who gave me another number. But they said if I'm not eight weeks they can't do anything about it.'

'What do you mean?'

'I don't know. The scan won't pick it up, or something.'

'How far along are you?'

'I don't know. About six, I think.'

'Did you tell them that?'

'No, I said I didn't know.'

'So what have they told you to do?'

'Just to wait, and if it gets bad, to ring back.'

'Have you got any appointments today?'

'A few.'

'Why don't you cancel them?'

'I need the money for a start, but I'll just be sitting here worrying.' Her voice began to tremble. 'What if I'm losing my baby?'

<h1 style="text-align:center">26</h1>

abies had become the focus of my world. They were coming at me from all angles of life. Maybe it was an indication that I was doing the wrong thing. I'd woken up from another nightmare sweating because I'd been taking my baby for a walk but I was naked except for a child's vest top. I gave up trying to sleep when every time I closed my eyes I was faced with my nudity. Apparently, in the world of dreams nakedness means feelings of insecurity. I knew this because I'd had plenty of these dreams when I was younger. Especially after Mum was gone. I would dream that Dad had sent me to school with only my knickers and vest on, or that I was completely naked. It was a customer who informed me of its symbolic connotation; all dreams, she'd told me, have one.

I decided to get up. I couldn't cope with symbols, images and the whole meaning behind the language of my dreams. I knew what the problem was. I'd been side-tracked into following a whole new life-plan, a whole new journey, and my unconscious was still trying to catch up.

Max was sleeping next to me. It was nice having him in my bed. I loved that we were embarking on this new adventure together. We'd agreed that once we'd had the scan we would start to move my stuff over to his house. I was glad that he'd redecorated, as any traces of Gina may have had me putting the house up for sale. I couldn't decide whether to rent the flat out, or expand the salon upstairs. My thoughts were swirling at the moment, especially as I had to put Libby somewhere. I'd still not told her our plans.

I checked my phone. There was no text from Suzy but it was only 7.23a.m. I was surprised the hospital had told her to phone back on a Saturday if she was still worried. But she'd said it was the emergency Maternity Day Unit. I suppose dealing with babies isn't a Monday to Friday, 95 job.

When I spoke to her the night before she'd said there had been no more bleeding, or spotting as she was referring to it; apparently the medical term. She was constantly finding out more from the things she was reading. I hadn't picked up a book, a magazine or a leaflet, although I didn't need to with Suzy giving me a running commentary on our 'babies' development'. She said that our babies' facial features would be developing by six weeks; there would be black spots where the eyes were forming. There would be little arm buds and nostrils and ears marked with tiny openings. There would be a heartbeat. 'Can you imagine, Kat, a little heartbeat?'

The problem was, I *could* imagine. Her description of the bean-size egg I'd been thinking about instantly became a real-life being. A being who was breathing and alive. I had caught my breath in my throat and tears had rolled down my cheeks.

It was real; this baby would be joining us soon, I ought to start finding out what I would have to do. I wondered if there was a course on bonding with your child, or even something a bit simpler, such as '*What to do with a baby, from start to finish.*' I could have done with a full-time nine-month lesson plan on what the hell I was supposed to be doing.

Suzy had also told me to stop drinking so much coffee, as a high caffeine intake is connected to miscarriages and sudden infant death syndrome. So I poured myself a cup of lemon tea.

'See, if you weren't telling me this stuff, I wouldn't have a clue,' I'd told Suzy. 'How do other pregnant women know?'

'Well, I think most women who fall pregnant are trying, so they've probably read the books and know their stuff. Plus, you forget not everyone *does* live on caffeine.'

'Okay, normal people do,' I'd jested.

Suzy didn't live on caffeine, she said it wasn't needed. 'If you have your diet, exercise and lifestyle right your energy will fall into place.' All I heard was, 'Blah, blah, blah.' I was amazed that we'd stayed friends, despite being so different in so many areas of our lives.

At last a text arrived from Suzy indicating all was okay. She would see how today went, but the spotting had stopped. I was relieved. It felt great that we were going through this together; she'd been so made up when I'd told her we were keeping the baby. Everyone around me thought I was doing the right thing. 'It's fate,' Suzy had said. 'It's probably your mum's gift to you.'

'I'd have been happy with shoes,' I'd replied.

I prepared myself for the day ahead, Saturday being our busiest day. Mandy was coming to join us; she'd been such a great support. She had her own customers already and was becoming quite busy, so the salon expansion was moving in the right direction. The more I thought about it, I knew transforming the flat would be the best thing to do. It would give us so much more space. I felt excited about the prospect of having a larger salon.

Max left, and not long after I went down to the salon. He was training with Joe and Lawrence. The triathlon was only a few weeks away.

'Two weeks today,' Melanie said as she burst through the door, 'I'll be a nervous wreck.'

I'd had this for the past two months, every Saturday a countdown to her wedding. I'd never closed the salon on a Saturday before, but there was no way I was missing her wedding. I couldn't cope with not seeing the final show after I'd lived through it for the past eighteen months.

'So exciting,' I said, as I said every Saturday morning.

She talked for the next five minutes about the wedding, what she still had to do, what others had to do, how she'd managed to squeeze in the extra five people (the long-lost uncle and his family: wife and three kids). I nodded and contributed in the right places. I couldn't wait for this wedding to be over.

After I'd treated my first lady to a facial, I left her to organise herself and meet me at the desk, as I did with all my customers.

I was greeted with a huge bouquet of fresh flowers, which sat vibrantly on the reception area.

'Someone's gonna get lucky tonight!' Melanie laughed with her customer.

I read the label, which was displayed in the middle of the flowers. 'I love you xxx very much xxx.' I felt my heart swell. I was so lucky. I felt like the most loved woman in the world. How could I have doubted that he loved me? I excused myself so I could put the flowers upstairs once my customer had left.

As I entered the flat I could smell something sweet. I wondered if Libby had lit a joss stick, but then realised I didn't have any left. Music played from her bedroom. I shouted her but there was no reply. I shouted again but still no answer. Placing the flowers on the table in the middle of the sitting area, I headed to her room.

'Lib.' I knocked on her door, opening it slightly, smoke gently drifted passed me. 'Lib, are you okay?' I heard scuffling and whispering, then I saw Calvin, or whatever his real name was.

'Oh, hello!'

'Hi.' Calvin slurred his words and Libby started to giggle.

I realised they were sitting on something, hiding something from my view. 'Libby, what's going on?'

'Nothing,' she said, starting to laugh again. 'Oh, for fuck's sake, Kat, you're not my mother, now get out of my room.'

'*Your room?*' My voice was rising as I walked towards them. Libby tightened her grip on whatever was under the covers. 'This is my home you're staying in rent bloody free.'

'Here she goes with her—' I didn't let her finish as I grabbed her hand. Calvin moved out of the way, his face white as he held onto the bed.

'I think I'm going to be ....' He threw up all over the floor. It hit the walls, the wardrobe, the desk, the curtains, the ornaments, the bedding ... you name it, his insides were now hanging from it.

'Oh Jesus, Cal, are you okay?' Libby's eyes rolled as she spoke.

'Oh my God, get out of my house!' I screamed.

'Come on, let's get out of here, until she calms down.' Libby grabbed his arm. I thought he might pass out but I was so enraged I didn't care. If he passed out here, I'd have to deal with him. Outside, he was her problem, or someone else's.

'Libby, you'd better find somewhere else to live. You're not welcome back here.' I felt icy calm as the words passed my lips. I'd never thought I'd ever see my sister on the streets, but I couldn't have her here anymore. 'I won't let you take advantage of me, Libby. Drugs in my house. You disgust me.'

She didn't reply as she left.

I was fuming. I was so infuriated, I was shaking. I opened the bedroom window to clear the smell then closed the bedroom door, because my next client was due. I didn't have time to sort the mess out.

I needed to calm down before I went back downstairs. I could tell Melanie what had just happened but I didn't want my customers knowing. I hoped no-one had seen Libby and her friend when they were leaving.

Oh God, what had I done? I'd chucked my sister out. What would Mum have said to that? But I couldn't let Libby back in. If I did, she would walk all over me forever. I couldn't let that happen. She was on her own.

But instead of feeling free, I felt another burden fall upon my shoulders.

27

It was the phone call later that day that sent my world into a rollercoaster of more upheaval.

'Kat, you need to come to the hospital.' Marianne was obviously distressed and her words filled me with dread. I knew what had happened.

At the hospital we all fell silent as the doctor spoke to us. Libby's tears formed and she blinked them away. I placed my hand on hers. Icy chilled fingers entwined as we connected. I wanted to say, 'Don't worry, I'll be here for you.' I wanted to hug her, tell her we'd done it before and we could do it again. But I didn't have the strength.

He was gone.

I'm not sure what was worse, waiting for it to happen or it happening suddenly. I tried to digest the information, I tried to understand. I'd known this might be the ending but at the same time I was waiting for our dad to come back to us. The dad from years ago, who laughed, enjoyed life and loved us. I'd been waiting for him. I thought he would appear. I really thought it would happen. I really thought he would have found the strength to fight for us. I knew he was lost in his own world, a world which no-one understood, but I thought he would leave that world and come back.

I'd always hoped that one day he would wake up and take the steps needed. But now, that chance was gone. He'd given up. I knew, though, this was his ultimate plan. He'd be laughing. I was hoping he was with Mum; they'd found each other and it was like it used to be. If that was the case, I was happy for them. But why did it hurt so much? Why did I feel as if someone was ripping me apart? Why did I feel that this couldn't be happening? I didn't know how to handle it. How to grieve for the man I knew, but didn't know. The man he had become was like an unknown figurine, a statue in a stale house leading a meaningless life. I would grieve for the man I missed, but he had been gone a very long time.

As we sat in the room alone after the doctors had explained the next steps, I thought about my child. My baby. I'd heard that depression was an illness; what if my child was to inherit it? What if I couldn't help? Like I couldn't help Dad. I'd always thought it had been triggered by Mum's death, but what if it had started before that? I had no-one to ask.

We'd decided to have this baby, but what if something happened to me? What if something happened to Max? What if something happened to both of us? Where would our baby go? Would Clare take time out from her social diary? Would Marianne take on the role? Would Libby or Suzy contribute? Would I want this?

I wanted to sleep. I wanted to disappear. I needed some distance, some time to think clearly as I couldn't think straight.

I left Marianne and Libby at the hospital. I didn't ask where Libby was staying; I assumed it would be with Marianne but I didn't ask. I didn't want to give her the option of coming back. It had taken me over an hour to clean up the mess. Curtains and bedding in the wash, the walls cleaned, but the carpet was stained. His dirty habit engrained in my home forever. I was so angry with Libby, though with Dad's death I wanted to hug her, keep her close like I'd always done.

I drove to Max's, needing to grieve. I just wanted him.

That evening, I cuddled up to him and sobbed. I poured out all the emotions I had left for Dad. Every tear was sorrow for the life he'd lived. Not because he'd passed away, but because his life had become worthless. He was in the place he wanted to be sixteen years ago. I tried to imagine him smiling, laughing like we had that day. It helped me sleep, as Max took me into his arms and hugged me like he'd never let me go.

My last thoughts before I slept were of the day I last saw my dad: at Lampford Park.

I stayed with Max all day Sunday. Clare understood we didn't want to come for dinner. She was so pleased we had 'worked things out'. If only Max knew how much I had to thank her for. I couldn't tell him without betraying her confidence, which I didn't want to do.

I'd spoken with Marianne. I could hear Libby in the background. I was pleased she was there. I'd tried to push her from my thoughts but it wouldn't happen. She was still my sister, whether or not I agreed with what she was doing. I'd looked out for her over the last sixteen years; quashing that instinct was hard. I didn't want her back in my flat, though, cruel as it may sound. She was safe at Marianne's. I could sleep at night with a clear conscience, knowing she was there.

Marianne had asked if I would mind if Dad was brought back home in an open coffin before the funeral. I thought it was a strange request. I knew some people preferred to say their goodbyes this way, but I wasn't sure who would want to say goodbye to Dad. It's sad, but he didn't have any friends. The family that there was had all disappeared into the background. Dad's family had never been on the scene. His mum and dad had passed away when I was young and before Libby was born. He had two brothers, but they'd never stayed in contact after their parents had died. Even the traditional Christmas card, just to show willing, had diminished. It's amazing how one person's death can rumble through a family, knocking people out like a game of skittles.

I often wondered about the young lad who was driving the car that hit Mum's car; the young lad who'd caused this misery. He'd be in his thirties. I wondered if he had his own family, his own children and if his life had been as hard as ours. But I would stop myself, as it didn't help anyone to analyse over and over again.

Marianne said the open coffin would have been what Dad wanted. I was sure Dad wouldn't have cared where he was. I thought she needed him in the house. He wasn't much use when he was here, she'd told me, but she wanted his presence. I hadn't argued with her. I didn't care where his body was. I wasn't being disrespectful but to me it was only his shell.

I stayed with Max on Sunday night and we relished each other's company. We talked about how our lives would change. I complained a little that I would have to get up at least fifteen minutes earlier to get to work, when I moved in with him. He'd laughed. 'Fifteen minutes? You wait: when this baby comes, fifteen minutes will be nothing.'

We'd asked the midwife to come to Max's house, because that was where our baby would be starting its new life. Max made us breakfast; although I was still struggling to get anything down on a morning, I knew it always made me feel better when I had. He also made me tuna sandwiches for my lunch. He put me a little box together, which I thought sweet and romantic. He said it had to be tuna because apparently it was a prerequisite of a pregnant woman's diet. 'However,' he said, 'you must be careful not to have more than two medium-sized cans or two fresh tuna steaks a week.' (He'd been reading the pregnancy books and a few magazines too. I'd also bought him *The Bloke's Guide to Pregnancy* by Jon Smith. It was my way of saying, 'I'm not doing this on my own!') Max mumbled something about the mercury levels in fish and that I should avoid shark and swordfish. *Since when has shark and swordfish been part of our regular diet?* I didn't ask him because he was trying so hard, it felt cruel to mock him.

Luckily the midwife was on time. This pleased me as I'd only left space for a morning out of the salon. Max had also cleared his diary for the morning. We were both very nervous. This was unknown territory for us.

The midwife introduced herself as Pam. She was a plump, older lady with ash-blonde hair, easily mistaken for white, cut to her shoulders in a trendy feathered bob. Her smile was genuine and warm, her cheeks displaying a hint of pink. She'd obviously been doing this job for years. Her confident but warm manner was soothing. I was pleased she wasn't a trainee, although I wasn't sure if trainees did the initial visit. Not that there's anything wrong with trainees; as I've said before, we've all got to start somewhere. But I didn't have a clue what I was doing and I didn't need someone who wasn't quite sure either, checking their text books for corroboration.

I took her into the sitting room, whilst Max made the coffees and a tea for me. Pam chose the single chair, which enabled her to face us, her briefcase by her side. 'Right.' She clasped her hands together, resting them on her knee against her blue uniform. I noticed the watch hanging from her pocket and wondered if it worked; I'd thought it was only something nurses wore for show on the TV. 'Okay, so what I've got to do today is go through quite a few questions. Obviously, if you have any, this is a good time to ask.'

My first was, 'Do you have all day?' She laughed. I was serious.

'So how have you been feeling?' She reminded me of Mum. I liked her. She made me feel warm and childlike, in a safe, secure way. Strange, really, considering I'd just met her.

'Really tired and sick and I'm not sure how I can make the sickness go.' I didn't explain about Dad; it was a story I didn't want to get into.

'Unfortunately, there isn't a cure. Have you tried ginger biscuits?'

'Yes, they didn't work.' I tried hard not to say it through gritted teeth, or swear. I was tired of people telling me to eat ginger biscuits.

'Are you eating okay?'

'I'm trying to. I'm getting better. I *have* struggled over the last few weeks.'

She told me to keep an eye on things, as we needed to make sure the baby was getting the correct nutrition. The tiredness, she informed me, was extremely common, unfortunately part of pregnancy and motherhood. Great! Then she flicked through her file, asking us basic questions: our names, dates of births, careers and other facts that helped her understand what type of family we were. When she asked, 'Was the pregnancy planned?' and didn't look up, expecting us to say yes like most couples probably did, we both fell silent. We glanced at each other in desperation.

'So I'm assuming this wasn't planned?' She looked at us inquisitively. I felt like a small child being told off at school. Her hands rested on her clipboard, her stare intense.

Oh God, they'd get the social workers in, they'd take our baby away. I felt a stab of something, I'm not sure what; fear, maybe. Could this be a good sign, a maternal instinct of some kind kicking in? 'Well, the thing is,' I started as if I was going to invent an excuse, 'Max and I weren't really planning on having children … just yet. As I mentioned on the phone, it was all a bit of a shock.'

'Right.' She nodded, as if she understood. 'So, how do you feel now?'

'Very excited,' Max piped up. I looked at him. His acting skills were not up to scratch. Pam seemed to be studying my reaction, so, turning back and smiling at her, I found myself nodding in agreement with him.

'Okay.' She didn't look convinced. I could feel her eyes piercing, burning through me. Uncomfortably I shifted in my seat. 'And what about you, Kathryn? How do you feel?'

I hesitated. I didn't know what to say. I couldn't let Max down, but I couldn't be all fluffy with excitement about something that sent fear through me every time I thought about it. Pam seemed to understand that I was searching for the right words, but Max had turned to stare at me, panic pasted across his face. He rubbed my back, to comfort me. Perhaps he also wanted to push his hand up the back of my shirt and work me like a puppet.

'I'm still getting used to the idea. But we're happy. I'm happy. But it's all been a shock, really.'

'That's understandable.' She made a note on her pad. I imagined her scribbling, 'DANGER – MOTHER UNFIT. TAKE CHILD AT BIRTH.'

'I'm not against it, though.' Had she interpreted me wrong? Did Max think I hadn't helped our situation? 'We are happy.'

'Great.' She smiled, as if reading my mind. 'Being pregnant can be very tough, especially when you feel tired and sick. Don't worry, it can take a while to understand the pressures and once you do, the baby will be here and you will have so many other little worries.' She laughed and we politely laughed with her, but I thought about the tons of worries I already had, let alone piling on any more. I didn't even know the basics, like changing a nappy, feeding, cuddling and talking nonsense. I was worried about the sleepless nights, teething and nappy rash that my clients talked about. I would have quite happily lived my life not having to deal with this.

She reeled off lots of questions about family diseases, blood groups and other matters, to which we replied, 'Don't think so,' or, 'Yes, probably.' I didn't really know who in my family had a bad heart or bone disease. The interview, I'm calling it that because that's what it felt like, lasted an hour. When Pam left I felt a sense of relief. Although she was lovely and I did warm to her, it had been gruelling. She had said she was going to push along our scan, so we could get a better idea of dates, but from her calendar I could be around twelve weeks, so we needed the scan very soon.

So it was all happening. The midwife had been. The ball was rolling. I would be registered at the hospital as a pregnant woman. I was going to be a mum. Me! Oh God, what if I messed up? Max wrapped me in his arms and told me it was going to be okay. And for some reason, I believed him.

I drove back to the salon, music and chatter from the radio filling the car. The windows were down, the sun was beaming, my sunglasses blocking out the strong rays. I thought about my poor dad, but I tried to focus on how happy he must be feeling now. It was all over for him; the pain and torture of living was over. But still a lump formed at the back of my throat, threatening to bust.

My phone sang out to me as Suzy's face beamed back at me, helping to divert my thoughts. 'Hiya,' I answered.

'Kat, I think it's happening.' She sounded urgent through my hands-free speaker.

'What is?'

'I'm losing the baby.'

29

The Maternity Day Unit was a smaller part of the hospital, situated along a corridor behind the maternity reception desk, shut away from the labour rooms, shut away from the outside where pregnant women congregated for a sly cigarette. We noticed two women chatting, dressed in thin dressing gowns and pyjamas. One of them was saying that she was worried her baby was too small, as they puffed away on the nicotine sticks. Suzy looked at me, raising her eyebrows, I shook my head as we passed by them.

Through the double doors was a small desk that represented the reception area. A younger midwife greeted us, introducing herself as Fiona. I wondered if she had children. But she looked too young to have children and to be a fully qualified midwife. Could she possibly have squeezed all that in? You never know, these days. She wasn't wearing a wedding ring. I told myself to stop looking for these pointless pieces of information. Her blonde hair was tied back tight off her face, a small bun gathered at the nape of her neck and a fringe trimmed neatly just above her eyes. She looked professional and trustworthy. She was very friendly, which helped, unlike the older midwife, who kept snapping from the back room about files not being left in the right order.

Fiona ignored the background noise, concentrating on Suzy as she wrote down some of her essential information. Suzy explained how she'd had some spotting a few days ago. It had seemed to stop, but there was a lot more that morning. Fiona nodded and asked how far on she was. Suzy admitted that she thought about six weeks. Fiona told us they didn't normally scan until after eight weeks because it was sometimes hard to pick anything up. (We knew she'd say this, and I'd told Suzy to add a few weeks on. But she couldn't lie.) If that was the case she advised Suzy not to panic, but it could mean coming back to reassess the situation. After the formalities were completed for Suzy's admittance, she pointed to the tiny waiting room, which could only fit seven or eight visitors. We sat opposite a couple who looked comfortable; not anguished, not upset, but settled. The woman looked happily pregnant. I guessed she was about six months on, but really I didn't have a clue. Although the couple seemed content, they weren't talking, just staring at the television in the corner.

Suzy handed me a magazine and chatted aimlessly about Victoria Beckham and Cheryl Cole, who were on the front. I knew she was trying to keep her mind off the reality of her situation. I felt so sorry for her. I was the only person she could rely on. She still hadn't told her mum and if this was the end of Suzy's pregnancy, then it was best to leave her mum out of it.

It was about half an hour before Fiona came back. She nodded for Suzy to follow her. I told Suzy I'd wait here for her. She seemed okay with that but she looked lost. I found this department quite daunting. I watched the midwives chat amongst themselves about patients' notes. Posters across the walls encouraged help in different departments: child-rearing, ante-natal classes, post-natal depression, breast-feeding. It all felt a bit too much. I walked around, breathing deeply, as if I'd attended one of these classes already. I wanted to compose myself before Suzy came back. She needed me to be the strong one.

Ten minutes, and she was back. Red-eyed and snivelling into some torn pieces of tissue. I hugged her close. We didn't say anything as she wept quietly into the neck of my black tunic. I didn't know what to say. Why was life so unjust sometimes? Suzy didn't deserve this; whereas look at me, blocking out what most people would believe was the most magical thing on earth.

Suzy explained later that the baby had actually disintegrated. I'm not sure if that was the medical term, but that's how she described it. She told me that the sac was still attached to the womb but there was no baby inside. At some stage it could all come away. This could take up to three weeks or longer, but the quicker option was to go back to the day unit and take the medication that would make everything happen quickly.

The sac was still attached to the womb but there was no baby inside. The words kept repeating themselves in my mind. The shell of what she wanted was attached to her, but the soul of what she wanted was no longer available to her. I thought of Dad as the sac surrounding the soul, but the soul was no longer there. These two lives connected: Dad's, and Suzy's baby's. Both lives full of potential but cut short because they lacked the necessary requirements to survive.

'Do I tell him?' She covered her face with her hands. I was driving her home. Mandy had stayed longer at the salon and I said I would be there when I could. Having Mandy had become a God send. I wasn't sure how we'd coped before without an extra pair of hands.

'Does he deserve to know?' I spoke softly, not really knowing what she should do. My ability to give advice seemed to have gone into some kind of dysfunctional melt down since I'd lost control of my own life.

'No, probably not.' It was almost a whisper. 'Can you come with me?' Her quietness made her sound like a child.

I nodded and said, 'Of course.' How was I going to manage this? I was fully booked; my clients were back-to-back. Suzy was due to go back to the hospital the following morning to take some pre-medication, and 'it' would happen on Wednesday. But I couldn't say no. She looked desperate. Who else could she ask? Also, I didn't want her to go through it on her own. I would be there. I would rearrange the diary, see if Mandy could help us. I would sort things out to be with Suzy.

I dropped her off at home, kissed her cheek and we hugged for a while. I told her everything happens for a reason and that I was sorry; all those things we say to make people feel better.

It didn't work.

I knew she was thinking the same as me, that I had everything she wanted. I had a baby growing inside me. I had a man who supported and loved me and we were building a new life together, embracing the addition that would be joining us soon. I had everything Suzy wanted and I didn't deserve it. Like Suzy didn't deserve to lose her child.

'It should have been me,' I whispered gently. She kissed my cheek, wiped away a tear and thanked me before leaving the car. Not agreeing, nor disagreeing.

But I knew she felt the same.

30

The coffin had arrived in Dad's home. I felt a desperate need to stay away but at the same time a need to see him. I felt I'd already said my goodbyes, but it would be rude not to visit. When I arrived after work, the street looked the same as it always did. I don't know why I'd been expecting it to look any different.

The walk into Dad's gloomy house seemed endless. My feet felt as heavy as lead, as I dragged them up the path. I didn't want to go in. I didn't want to be there. 'He's your father,' I kept telling myself. I wondered if Mum was pressing some kind of automatic button in my brain, as the message was being drilled repeatedly into me.

Entering the house was like entering a black hole. There was no atmosphere except a depressing sadness. Marianne appeared in the hallway when she heard me enter. Smiling sadly, she pulled me close. I responded, as I thought she needed it more than me.

'You okay?' she asked me.

'I'm fine.' I smiled. 'You?'

She nodded. 'He's in the lounge.' She said it like she always said it. 'Why don't you go and pop your head in? He's just resting. I'll put the kettle on.'

Had she lost the plot? He's just resting? My skin crawled with goose-bumps. I shivered at how she was describing his presence in the house. I wanted to shout, 'He's dead.' But I don't think she wanted to hear that.

I walked towards the room where he always sat, drink in hand. Marianne had tried hard to make the place look homely, placing random plastic and fresh flowers at the bottom and top of the stairs. The shrine of pictures covered the cream embossed wallpaper, which was heavily stained and in serious need of replacing. I felt queasy and took a step back, holding onto the old rickety staircase, grabbing at a spindle as I felt the rush of nausea swarm over me like a flock of birds searching for their next feed. The once cream spindles were in definite need of another coat or two of paint. Two were missing like old decayed teeth. I leaned against the wall, listening to it creak under my weight. It sounded like a musical melody that was out of tune. The bathroom, which was situated directly under the staircase, had the door slightly ajar, because it didn't have a lock on it. The rule, as always, was: if the door is slightly open it means nobody is in there; if the door is shut it means the bathroom is in use. Dad was never in any fit state to fix it, Marianne had no idea where to start and Libby and I just became accustomed to it. I wondered how many other families had such oddities in their house. Max definitely didn't.

Breathing deeply, I moved forward, trying to pull myself together. I took hold of the brass door handle and entered. Usually if the living room door was closed we followed a protocol: don't knock, just quietly enter (another unwritten rule). Then a quick check to see if Dad was okay and make sure he hadn't done anything dramatic. It was too late for that now; he'd done it. I must admit that when I moved out this was something I didn't miss; wondering what to expect behind the closed door.

Dad lay in the coffin. He didn't look like himself. The embalmers had done a great job and he looked better than he did when he was alive; but he didn't look the way he used to. I sat on a chair which had been placed deliberately by his coffin. I wondered how many times Marianne had sat here today. It felt strange, weird, to be sitting next his body, although this is what it had always felt like when he'd passed out from drinking too much.

I'd never really taken much interest in the house. As I studied the room in which Dad lay, I realised how shabby the place was. Worn, deep-purple fabric hung at the windows. Marianne had obviously tried, but I couldn't say she'd made a good effort. They were all frayed at the sides and along the bottom, the carpet was thread bare in random places, the dark wooden furniture was chipped, like the kitchen table.

She had placed a quilt over Dad. I assumed it was his bedroom quilt, to keep him warm, make her feel he was still with her. Even the quilt, which was once white, was now a musky grey colour. It displayed washed-out flowers in reds, yellows, oranges, blues and pinks, which had blurred as if hiding in the background. Nothing matched in the room. Even the ornaments were oddly placed. A petite white vase stood elegantly on the sideboard at the back of the room, containing two porcelain flower heads, each of which had lost at least one petal. Next to the vase stood a large figure, a wooden Indian man with his hands on his hips and a determined glare on his wooden face. His stance was creepy. He used to be in Dad's bedroom. I wondered if there was an important meaning behind him and that's why he was joining Dad now. Marianne probably thought there was a spiritual element to him. She probably believed he was looking after Dad.

As I looked around the tatty room, I knew I was being unfair. There was nothing contemporary about the way they lived and the house would definitely never have featured in *Homes and Gardens,* but it was always clean and tidy. Money was short and Marianne had tried to make the place come alive with ornaments and flowers, and give a perception of a composed and organised life style. Similar to how she presented *herself* really. Similar to how *I* presented *myself.*

I watched Dad's peaceful face and wondered what he'd thought about his living conditions, compared to the nice family house we'd had before Mum died. They were both happy in their work, happy in their lives; and it was all taken away from him. No wonder he spent most of his time drinking. By the time I was old enough to realise what was happening to him, it was too late. I couldn't help him. I wished I had some magical powers that would make him come back a changed man, the man he used to be. I'd have made Mum come back too.

I wanted to make this sadness go away.

I wanted to be able to talk to him about the pregnancy. I wanted to analyse our thoughts together. I wanted him to be thrilled to be a granddad. I held his thin, bony hands and felt the tears stinging, my throat becoming dry and thick. I swallowed back the heavy lump, trying to stop the tears erupting. I sat in silence, but it was so frustrating. I wanted him to talk to me, tell me why. Why had he chosen to take this route? Why had he given up so easily? He had me and Libby, didn't he? 'Why?' I whispered silently. 'Why, Dad?' But he didn't move.

There was no flickering of the eyes, no twitching of the arms, there was nothing. What did I expect?

Stroking his hand, I felt warmth surround me. My poor dad, my poor, tired dad, who wasn't old or incapable, he was weary, broken-hearted and fed up of this world. Fed up of being someone he didn't want to be.

Suddenly finding it hard to breathe, I left quickly, closing the door.

He was gone. He'd made his choice. I hoped he was in a happier place.

31

Marianne was waiting in the kitchen. A cup of coffee that had lost its steam awaited. Its strong smell was unbearable and turned my stomach. I didn't want to offend Marianne as she pushed it towards me, but I couldn't sit with it staring at me either. 'I don't want it, thanks.'

'Are you sure, Kat?' She had that look again, the one that made me think she could see through me, read my mind.

'I'm fine. Honestly,' I said. 'Where's Libby?'

'She went out. I'm not sure she's comfortable with your dad being here.'

Suddenly, in this awful situation, I wanted to laugh. I could imagine Libby freaking out about Dad 'resting' downstairs whilst she was trying to sleep at night. The stuff she'd been taking lately combined with a dead body in the house was probably not a healthy recipe.

'You know I'm here if you need anything or you want to talk about anything,' Marianne said quickly, her hands wrapped around her mug.

'You know, don't you?'

'Yes.'

'Did Libby tell you?'

'No, I knew when you called a few weeks back.'

'How?'

'I could just tell.' She smiled. 'Your face has changed. I just knew.'

'Oh.' I couldn't think of anything to say. I heard women talking about this in the salon. I'd heard young women saying their mothers knew before they did. I didn't feel comfortable with

Marianne knowing this about me, without having been told: she wasn't my mother.

'Everything will be okay. You know that, don't you?'

'I don't know anything at the moment, I feel lost.' I closed my eyes and rubbed my hands across my face. Why bother pretending? She'd known me long enough to know I'd be lying if I was skipping around her kitchen, shouting about this being the best thing that could have happened.

'Look, I've got a story to tell you. Would you like to hear it?' She spoke softly. I nodded because, unexpectedly, I *did* want to hear. I hoped for a fairy tale where the princess lived happily ever after. 'Well, I've lost two babies.'

Okay, maybe a real-life tale that would bring me back down to earth.

'It was before I met your dad.' She smiled a sad, weary smile, obviously remembering her pain. 'First was a miscarriage at fourteen weeks. A year later Thomas was born, four weeks early. He didn't make it.'

'I'm sorry,' I said. I thought of Suzy: would she tell people in years to come that she'd lost a baby? Would she describe her miscarriage in the terms Marianne had used? I'd thought of my baby as a bean in these early stages. A stab of remorse and shame pierced through me.

'No, it's okay. We're talking over sixteen years ago. Don't get me wrong, I think about him every day. Not a day passes me by when I don't wonder what he could have been and how my own life could have been very different.'

'In what way?'

'Well, I loved your dad to pieces, but it's not been easy.'

'We know.'

'When I first came to your home, I adored you two girls; you especially, Kat,'

'Really?' My forehead creased as if she had said something totally outrageous. 'But I was horrible to you.'

'You were a young, disturbed teenager who had lost her mum.' She paused and took hold of my hand. I felt my back stiffen a little. We'd opened up something which I was unsure of and now that Mum had been mentioned, guilt washed over me like a force.

'I never wanted to replace your mum, Kat.' Was this true? I couldn't bring myself to speak. I didn't know what to say to her without calling her a liar.

'Look, I was in a bad place myself when I came here, but I felt that I could help you girls and help your dad. When Thomas died and we held a little funeral, it was the worst time of my life. I thought I was going to die. I was having panic attacks. I couldn't stop crying. My husband was terrible. He didn't understand; he had so many issues himself. He was violent. He was a very angry man.'

'I didn't know you were married.' But then, I'd never asked. Not about her previous status. I'd never really asked her anything about herself. Showing an interest would have been betraying Mum.

'Well, I've never really got divorced.'

'You're still married?'

'No, he's dead now. He died about ten years ago. Cancer.' Her tone was flat as she explained. 'Anyway, the doctor admitted me to St John's not long after Thomas died, before I killed my husband, myself or someone else.'

'The doctor admitted you?' I asked, not understanding this part of her story: St John's was the institution in which Dad had stayed before he arrived home with her. 'I thought you were a nurse there?'

'No,' Marianne laughed, then composed herself. 'What gave you that idea?'

'Don't know.' I didn't. I didn't actually know why I'd thought this. The assumption just made sense at the time, I suppose. She was so caring and loving towards us, I presumed this had been her previous role. Looking back, I'd even wondered if she'd been sacked for having a relationship with a patient. My young imagination.

'I was a patient. I discharged myself. I found your dad lovely. We talked about so much in those few days. Probably more than we've ever talked since. You and your family saved me, Kat. All I've ever wanted to do was return that favour to you and Libby. You're both very special girls and I love you both very much.'

Her words hung in the air and I felt a blanket of love surround me. Remorse for the years I'd wasted hating and dismissing her. I'd felt lost and excluded when Libby and Marianne were together in the hospital, as if I'd been a bully with Marianne the victim of my awful crime, whilst Libby wanted to protect her. I was entering into unknown territory. I'd never wanted Marianne's company, her comfort and definitely not her sympathy. It wasn't her fault Mum died, but who was she to benefit from our sadness? A stranger who waltzed into our lives and took over. But had she really been that bad? She always cooked us meals. She cleaned and washed our clothes. She kept the house clean and tidy. She cared for us. She wanted to be let in but Libby and I kept her at arms' length. Well, I did, Libby just followed my lead; she was too young to understand. She was a shadow in my footsteps. When we were younger she would talk to Marianne the way I did, which, embarrassingly, was quite rude. If Marianne tried to get close to Libby, I would pull Libby towards me. I'd thought she had some kind of plan to turn Libby against me, or turn us both against Mum. A shaft of guilt ran through me. Had I really been so awful to her? Contemptuous? Derisive? Had I really been so malicious?

'Why did you stay with my dad?' My voice was soft and I found it hard to speak. 'What about us? We've never shown you any interest. I don't understand why anyone would put themselves through that.'

'I loved him and he needed me, just like I needed him. Like I need you girls.' I noted the present tense when referring to me and Libby. *I need you girls.* A tear formed in her eye. She blinked it away, as she said, 'I truly believe I came into your life for a reason, as I believe you and your family came into mine.'

'But this hasn't been an easy life. I still don't understand why you stayed, or why you believe we should still be in your life.'

'I wouldn't be here on this earth if it wasn't for you girls and your dad.' I thought I understood where she was coming from; we'd been her focus because her reality was much worse. 'Look, Kat, I don't want to tell you what to do with your life. I wouldn't have listened to anyone who told me what to do all those years ago. Well, I didn't listen. I lost all my friends coming to live here.' She paused. I could see her realigning her thoughts back on track. 'But what I'm saying is, I believe everything happens for a reason. I believe your baby has been sent to you. Having a child is the most precious gift you could ever ask for.' She smiled. 'But as I said, I'm not here to tell you what to do.'

'You don't need to worry, I'm keeping the baby.'

'Really? This is wonderful news.' She hugged me. It felt strange that the term *wonderful* was being used whilst Dad's body lay in the other room. 'I think it's the right thing to do.'

'I'm scared,' I admitted.

'Many women are.'

'I know, but I'm worried about things I shouldn't even be thinking about.'

We'd come this far; there seemed no point in blocking her out anymore. I held my breath, unsure whether to continue opening Pandora's box. There had been an emotional connection which we'd never experienced before; something Marianne had pushed for, something I'd always turned away from. We'd reached a point of no return in our relationship and I didn't want to hurt her.

'Is it because you lost your mum?' she asked cautiously.

We'd never talked about Mum. Now, here was Marianne, asking me a direct question about her. Here she was, wanting me to open up. I didn't want to shut her out, now that we'd jumped over this massive hurdle. 'Losing Mum was the hardest thing. I'm scared I'll lose my child and feel that loss again.'

'That may never happen. But I can assure you, the love you'll feel for that child will outweigh that fear.' Her words sang in the air like Clare's. Women with secrets, women with passion, women who had been through so much; I had these wonderful, inspiring women surrounding my life. I'd been blocking them out, fighting them away and had felt that I would be betraying Mum if I loved another mother figure.

'I'm sorry, Marianne, I've been so horrendously awful to you over the years. Why you don't hate me is beyond me.'

'You're a special person, Kat. I couldn't hate you.'

We'd pushed aside a barrier that had sat between us for years and although it felt strange, it felt right. Marianne had always been a stranger to me. She'd been in my life but I didn't know her. But she'd known me.

'I'm sorry for your loss,' I said. I meant her babies, her husband and Dad. 'I'm sorry you felt so much pain and no one was there for you.'

'You were all here, in your own way.' She smiled, and looked towards the ceiling. 'I've always had my faith.'

As we sat at the table that had seen so much of this family's turmoil, for the first time I saw Marianne the way she was: a special person who I was lucky to have in my life. Before I left she hugged me. I could smell her strong scent, which reminded me of the time she first entered our lives. She must have bathed in the stuff, as it took over the whole house, but there comes a point where you're immune to smells when you've been surrounded by them for so long. The smell had embedded itself into every crack of the house, the furniture, the walls, the flooring. It was a smell I didn't even pick up anymore. But today the perfume hit me the way it had the day she walked in. I felt a lump in my throat threatening to burst, again. A stray tear escaped; my hand brushed it away just as quickly.

Marianne stroked my hair. 'I never wanted to replace your mum.' Her smile was genuinely warm, her eyes reflecting the affection. 'But I've always loved both you girls like daughters.'

32

After working my way through a banana at 5a.m. (yes, I was up this early because I'd had naked babies chasing me in my dreams, again) I'd had a slice of toast at 6a.m., cereal with milk at 7a.m., and I was still hungry when I picked Suzy up at 8a.m. I'd brought along a flask, which was filled with milk. I'm not usually a huge milk fan, take it or leave it, but of late while I was eating my way through the Corn Pops (another craving I'd had) the milk tasted delicious. It did to me what wine would usually do. My taste buds and smells had changed so much over the last few weeks; I'd even gone off cucumber. Its watery flavour had changed into something which I imagined dead grass tasted like.

I was dreading the day ahead. I was worried about Suzy; we didn't know what to expect and I didn't know what to say to comfort her. She wanted me there, no-one else but me. I felt guilty for being the only person she could rely on. I felt almost responsible for her loss. It really should have been me. The strange thing was, although these thoughts were rolling around in my mind I didn't wish it was me. I felt fortunate that it wasn't.

Suzy hadn't slept a wink. She looked so tired, probably the worst I'd ever seen her, and she'd had her moments: drunk, disorderly and desperately regretful. But she'd lost that glint in her eyes, her carefree persona. She was never as light-hearted or happy-go-lucky as Libby, but she was generally positive and upbeat. Today she was trying to hide her grief; her smile was there, but not really. I wondered how many people lived their lives this way. More than we probably imagined.

We drove in silence. I'd tried the small talk, but the one-word answers were unbearable. She wasn't being nasty; she just needed to deal with this in her own way. I knew that. I understood that. The need for her to know I was there for her was overwhelming and powerful. But I knew she would talk to me when she was ready.

Fiona, the midwife who'd attended to Suzy originally, smiled as if we were good friends when we entered the Maternity Day Unit. Suzy's file was already made up. Fiona scanned through it before taking us to a private room. A plain room with white walls, white lino floor and a white bed; it should have looked pure with all the whiteness but it felt grubby and used. I wondered how many other women had suffered in these four walls.

Fiona was showing Suzy the bathroom, advising her that if the pain became too much she was more than welcome to have a bath. It was a shared facility, so Suzy would have to inform the medical staff if she wanted one. To save on embarrassment, Fiona told us. Another white door led to a toilet. I was pleased it was separate as my bladder couldn't have coped if Suzy decided to sit in the bath for a few hours. Although we'd seen each other naked lots of times while changing in front of each other or undressing in a drunken stupor, I didn't think she'd want me hanging over her whilst she was bathing.

Fiona gave Suzy some pills. She said they were slightly different from the ones taken the previous morning. Suzy had done that visit herself. I'd asked if she wanted me to come but it was a quick appointment, to get the process started, they'd said. She'd said she'd be fine.

I watched her. She looked so lost and lonely. She must have felt so isolated walking in here yesterday on her own. I felt another pang of remorse, as I had no way of easing her pain.

Fiona hadn't given her a hospital gown. She was allowed to stay in her normal clothes, which, as most days, was a sporty fashionable tracksuit. I wondered if she'd worn it to train *him?* Would she throw it away after today? Wouldn't she think of this anguished day, full of suffering and distress, every time she looked at it?

Fiona left us to it, saying that she would keep calling in but that we were to have no hesitation in calling her. The process could take a few hours or it could take all day, and if nothing had happened by 7p.m. we would have to come back tomorrow. A slight feeling of panic arose. I pushed it away. Suzy was more important. I was sure Mandy wouldn't mind doing another day for me. I'd double-check with Melanie once Suzy was settled. I'd had to make some excuse about me visiting the hospital, as Suzy didn't want anyone to know.

'Milk is really good for the baby,' Suzy said as she lay on the bed and I sipped milk from my flask.

'Good, because I think I have my first craving, either that or I'm just addicted to the stuff.'

She smiled. I appreciated her mentioning my own pregnancy in the midst of what she was going through.

'Can you remember when you were addicted to sherbet dips?' she reminisced.

'Oh my God, you're right,' I laughed, encouraging her to think of other things. 'I loved the way they made my insides tingle. I couldn't bear it now.'

'Do you remember how we would get our penny mix-up before school?'

'Yes, we were allowed to get our own, until -'

'They realised that our twenty-pence mix-ups were more like fifty,' she said, smiling.

'That's theft, really. I'm surprised we weren't arrested.'

'We would be, these days.'

'Can you imagine all the kids being taken out of school?'

'I know, but you've got to think how much it must have cost that shop. If every kid in our school, or most of them, helped themselves to fifty pence of sweets instead of twenty every day, the shop was losing a fortune. I wonder how they managed to stay in business!' She looked at me. Her knees were bent and her arms were wrapped around them tightly. Her long blonde hair, which usually flowed around her shoulders, was caught up in a ponytail, showing her fresh face. She was so pretty, her skin flawless and the features well portioned, even the small row of stitches above her eye didn't distract from her beauty. But she looked tired. Drained.

'By counting all the sweets and making everyone feel like a criminal.'

'Do you know, though, the worst thing is, we didn't feel like criminals. That's terrible, isn't it?'

'God, my dad would have killed me!' I bit my lip and shook my head. A drunk and a depressive he may have been, but he was no thief. He would have been deeply ashamed of the thirty sweets I was gaining for free every day.

'Your dad? Bloody hell, could you imagine my mother?' Suzy said, trailing off as she said the word 'mother'. A silence filled the room, as Suzy looked away from me.

'Do you think you will tell your mum?'

She shook her head. 'There's no point; she'd be upset and I'd have to soothe her.' She smiled, then added, 'And I don't have the energy.'

'It will get better, Suz.'

'Yeah, I know.' She sighed heavily, as if she didn't really believe it.

A change of subject needed, we analysed how the petite television worked. A pre-paid card was required, a code to be entered to allow access. We sorted that, but it did prove difficult. Three attempts later we were staring at *Jeremy Kyle*. Suzy said she loved watching his shows, as it made her life feel not so bad. She was shaking her head as a young man strutted onto the stage; big, baggy jeans, a hooded top and a bald head. A younger girl, who was much larger than him in both width and height, then stood up quickly from her chair and tried to hit him. Jeremy wasn't having that type of behaviour. Suzy seemed happy to watch this young couple, so we listened to Jeremy helping them put their world to rights, after a few harsh but truthful words. I wondered what he'd say about my situation. Would he tell me to get a grip? Would he bawl me off the stage? Would he belittle Max in front of the live audience?

Marianne loved all this reality TV. She would even record episodes she might miss. I thought about Marianne and I told Suzy about my conversation with her. Suzy was thrilled. I felt pleased that she was happy for me. Not that I needed her approval, but she'd seen my life. She'd lived it with me. If she'd thought I was doing the wrong thing she would have told me.

I made sure she was comfortable while I went out to make a phone call to the salon. I checked she didn't need anything bringing back and asked if she was sure she was okay, repeatedly, until she practically shouted at me to leave the room.

Sophie answered, her sweet voice making her sound very young. Melanie spoke to me briefly, whilst her lady got dressed after her leg-waxing treatment. Mandy was being a Godsend, Melanie said. Although it was great that the salon was running smoothly, I hated not being a part of it. I was always part of it. It was my baby. Hmmm … my baby. It would no longer be my baby as such; I would have another baby to focus on. I would have to get used to the salon running without me.

Back in the room, Suzy was half reading a magazine while keeping an eye on the show. There was obviously no movement.

We sat in this tiny room, discussing the nurses who came in and out, the celebrities in the magazines, the people on the television. We analysed their lives and wondered what we would do in their situations. We were trying to distance ourselves but were both clock-watching.

It was 1p.m. when Fiona entered, handing Suzy more medication. It should happen in the next few hours, she told us. A small percentage of women had to go home, where many would pass the foetus, but a few would come back the following day. My instinct to protect Suzy stepped in; I told her that if it didn't happen this afternoon, she could stay at mine, or if she was more comfortable in her own home, I would stay there. Unexpectedly,

Suzy started to cry. She hadn't shed a tear all day, nor voiced a sad thought. I hugged her and she told me she was sorry. I didn't know why she should be.

'I didn't answer you,' she said, wiping the tears away. I knew what she was talking about. That moment she'd stepped from the car, the moment I felt as if I'd lost her and we would never connect properly again. 'It *shouldn't* be you,' she told me, as I'd wanted her to the other night.

'Why do I feel like it should?' I asked, bleakly.

'I don't know, but you shouldn't. Everything happens for a reason. How many times have we said that over the years?'

'Countless.'

'Well, there you go. My baby wasn't meant to be; yours is.' She smiled.

'You're so brave.'

'Nah, peed off and want to get out of here.' She smiled again through moist eyes.

Three hours later she was puffing and panting around the room. 'Fucking period pains, they said,' she growled through gritted teeth. I didn't know what to say. 'Fucking aspirin, fucking aspirin, what the fuck is that going to do?'

I was at a loss. I just kept telling her to breathe, as if she was in actual labour. And she looked like she *was*, holding onto the bed, closing her eyes, swearing under her breath. She was clearly in tremendous pain. It was awful because she didn't want me anywhere near her, she didn't want to be touched, she didn't want to speak, she just needed to get through this; and there was nothing I could do to help.

An hour of panting, swearing and begging a higher power to make it stop … it was over. She called for Fiona. Fiona checked.

It *was* over.

Physically over.

Emotionally and mentally I doubted it was over for Suzy.

I offered for her to stay at mine or that I would stay with her. But she declined, adding, no offence but she was exhausted and wanted to have a hot bath and go to sleep. She was worn out. She looked it. We kissed cheeks and hugged. 'Sorry' couldn't even begin to express how I felt for Suzy. As I spoke the word she shook her head and said, 'Reasons,' shrugging her shoulders. She thanked me for being there for her. To be honest, although I hadn't actually done anything I was shattered. I'd sat in a chair all day, coaxing my friend through one of the hardest days of her life; and I was so tired.

I watched her enter her house and wished there was someone inside to be with her. I didn't want her to be on her own. But at the moment she needed time alone. She wanted time alone.

At home Max was waiting for me. He'd cooked me a meal. I loved him for being there and caring enough to come to my flat rather than me making the extra journey to his. He explained he'd been out at a meeting, and instead of going back to the office he wanted to come and see if I was okay. He hugged me tight. My body felt fatigued, my heart felt full of weary emotion, helplessness and frustration. It should have been me, not Suzy. It felt so wrong; but it also felt so right that it wasn't me. I had to make this work. If not for me, for Max. For Suzy.

For our baby, who hadn't asked to be part of this world.

33

I pulled myself together, washed my face with warm water and stared at the reflection in the mirror. I had Dad's nose, small and neat, and his deep-brown, chocolate-coloured eyes, not like Mum's. Hers were green; they'd sparkled when she'd laughed. Libby had Dad's eyes too. Before he died a yellowish film had crept into the whites, but he looked so grey we'd hardly taken any notice.

I stepped from the bathroom, my black attire perfectly suited to the day's events. Dad's coffin lay in the back of the car that we all travelled in. Max stayed close beside me. I felt comfortable that he was helping me through this. Our final goodbye to Dad.

I didn't cry, neither did Libby. Marianne did, but she didn't make a scene. I felt I'd cried so much lately I had no tears left; my body had stopped producing them. I knew Dad was settled. He was at peace. He was where he wanted to be. I could analyse over and over how I could have made things better. I could tie myself in knots wondering how it had come to this. But the truth is, I couldn't have done anything differently. We can all look back on our lives, and ask, 'What if?' But it would stop us moving forward. I couldn't live in the past anymore. I'd lived in the past for too long, needing approval from Mum, blaming Marianne, being angry at Dad; and when it came to it, none of the emotional turmoil I'd put myself through had helped me.

I was surprised to see other people at his funeral. I realise that sounds cruel. But when I say other people, I mean the church was full. When we arrived, I was struck by the number of black suits, the number of people wanting to see him laid to rest. I didn't know these people. How did they know my dad? Who were they? I wondered if he'd led some secret life. I didn't even notice Suzy and her mum until we were leaving the church, as they were surrounded by all these unknown faces.

As we walked down the aisle following the coffin, I realised it was Marianne they were here for. Marianne was surrounded by so much love. They stroked her arm, some hugged her, some prayed with her: they were there for *her*. She had this community she'd created, a life outside Dad to keep herself going. How could she be so selfless? I thought of my child losing me and then being brought up by someone like Marianne; I was beginning to see that having Marianne in our lives was a blessing, not a hindrance. I felt so guilty. Mum definitely wouldn't have wanted me to behave in such an appalling manner towards Marianne. I'd have been chastised if Mum had seen some of the episodes I'd had with Marianne, who I now realised was a courageous woman and I was lucky to be part of her life.

In the graveyard, Dad was placed next to Mum. Among the muddy grass and headstones, they were surrounded by others whose lives had ended tragically or peacefully.

When it was over, when Dad had finally been laid to rest, we headed back to the house. A few of Marianne's friends followed, luckily not the whole church. They were lovely women who spoke of only good things, I thought it must be nice to be surrounded by such positivity and I understood how Marianne had coped. I also did something that day that I'd never done before: I offered Marianne a pamper day; a full body massage, facial and manicure. To many people, that might seem like nothing, but if Mum had been alive she would have been having treatments weekly. She would have been practically living there with me. Marianne understood this and her voice quivered, repeating, 'Thank you,' five times. We hugged and I felt so much affection towards her. A feeling I had never associated with Marianne. But it felt right. It felt so right.

Suzy, Libby, Max and I sat in the living room, like children at an adult gathering. Suzy's mum joined Marianne and her friends in the kitchen. I was glad they'd both come. Suzy's mum hadn't really seen Dad much over the years but she'd helped me through a lot when Mum died. It felt complete to have her with us. We were eating the cucumber sandwiches and cake that Marianne had prepared. I'd smiled at the tea party she'd crafted. Dad wouldn't have noticed; even less would he have cared; but these were things that Marianne enjoyed. These were the things I would learn to appreciate about her.

'So, I've been thinking,' Libby said.

'Did it hurt?' Max joked.

She smiled sarcastically at him. 'I'm going to go back to uni and do my teacher training.'

'Really?' I was overjoyed and couldn't keep the emotion to myself.

'Yes, it's the right thing to do.'

'I'm not forcing you, Lib, but I think it is.'

'But I'm going to stay here with Marianne. Are you okay with that?'

'Of course! I think it's a great idea.' I smiled, and I meant it. I thought about myself a few months back having this conversation with Libby; I'd have felt there was no reason to stay in touch with Marianne. I'd have kicked off and told Libby absolutely not, she must come back to live with me. I'd never seen Marianne as part of my life: she was part of Dad's and if he wasn't here, why would we be? But the change in my feelings was overpowering. It almost scared me. Marianne was someone I now realised I should be looking up to, someone I should admire and love.

I knew Dad would be proud. I knew Mum would be proud. I embraced my feelings of completeness and looked forward to the future with my new family.

34

Melanie looked stunning. Her gown hugged her figure and showed off the curves that Suzy had helped her create. A sweetheart neckline and low-cut bodice accentuated the flare of the pleated skirt. The back was tightly woven together with intricate beading, pulling her figure to its absolute shapeliest. It was plain, with hardly any embellishments, but its simplicity was exquisite. Family and friends gasped as she walked down the aisle.

It felt strange being in the same church. One week burying Dad, the following week celebrating a marriage. I'd realised the complexity of life was too much for me to keep analysing every twist. I'd visited Mum and Dad's graves before I'd come in, but I didn't feel a connection. They were surrounded by flowers from people who didn't even know Dad. Some had been placed on Mum's side. I thought it was sad that this might be the only place that some people could connect with their loved ones. I didn't feel as if either of my parents was actually there. I didn't visit Mum's grave much, for this reason. It wasn't because I didn't care but because it was her shell; I knew Mum was with *me*. She was with me always.

Once Melanie and Bobby had said their vows and happily kissed each other as man and wife, we all clapped, some people whistled, others shouted words of merriment; and it felt great to be surrounded by such cheer. We arrived at the hotel where the reception was taking place. Suzy travelled with me and Max. She'd had a 'plus 1' on her invite but didn't want to bring a guest. So we agreed we would go as a threesome. Max had joked about being the envy of all the men.

'Hiya mate, what you doing here?' Max said surprisingly, as he greeted his friend.

'Missed the bloody church, didn't I. Hope they didn't notice.' It was Lawrence. His tall, slim figure loomed as he shook hands with Max. The patted each other on the back, a macho stance. 'Hiya, Kat, how are you doing?' He reached down to hug me.

I stood on my tiptoes, although I was already in high heels, to greet him. 'I'm good, thanks. How are you?' I didn't see Lawrence that often, but when I did he was always so friendly. He always made me feel special as Max's girlfriend. He always made an effort to make sure I was okay.

'Well, I'm late for this wedding, but hey, if I walk in with you guys they won't notice.' He looked at Suzy. They'd never met before. Max and I had never really grouped our friends together and gone out for meals or drinks with them. 'Hi, I'm Lawrence, and who might this stunning girl be?'

'Suzy.' She laughed at his charm; it made him loveable. Her cheeks were tinged a little pink. I could have hugged him for showing her attention. With what she'd been through over the past few weeks, she needed a boost.

'Well, are you alone at this wedding?' He was playing his part very well and Max rolled his eyes at his friend's confident tactics.

'I am, kind sir,' Suzy flirted back with him.

'Well, shall we?' He held out his arm and she placed hers elegantly around it.

We walked together, as if we were a natural foursome.

'So why are you here?' Max asked, obviously wondering why Lawrence hadn't told him he was coming.

'I've been doing some consultancy with Bobby. I got a last-minute invitation and thought, why not?'

I remembered last week after Melanie had stressed about finding an extra five seats, because one of her aunties had split up from her uncle, so wouldn't be coming. She was harassed because she had to re-do the table plan. She'd already paid for his place and she mentioned that Bobby had been doing a lot of work with someone and he really wanted to invite him. She was miffed that it was now turning into a business conference rather than her wedding, but at least her uncle's place wouldn't be wasted.

Melanie had nothing to worry about: her whole day was perfect. Her mother, who was ensuring everything was going to plan, looked stunning in her bright orange attire. Sounds horrendous but it matched the bridesmaids'. She looked amazing. The whole bridal party looked amazing. I was so pleased that Melanie had taken the advice of so many brides who'd passed through the salon, about enjoying the day because it would be over so fast.

As the day moved into the evening, we watched Melanie and Bobby hold each other and move softly to their first dance. It had all been worth it, the tears and the screams: here she was, looking so happy. I'd helped her to re-apply her make-up just as I'd helped her that morning; rushing to her house before she squeezed into her wedding gown. She could have easily done it herself, but she was so nervous she was worried she wouldn't apply it right. I didn't mind. It was fun being part of the morning jovialities, drinking champagne (them, not me; okay, I had a small sip) and forcing Melanie to eat something. Her mum was lovely and I wondered why Melanie had been so stressed with her. 'We want it to be perfect,' she'd told me. I'd agreed, while thinking it all seemed a whole load of fuss.

But I didn't think that as I watched them embrace each other, kiss each other and show the world their love for each other. Lawrence came and joined us. We'd not seen him for most of the day; he'd been sitting with relatives. It appeared Melanie couldn't be bothered to re-do the table plan; she'd sat him where the uncle should have been. Lawrence being Lawrence, though, had flirted with the older women, who'd loved his charm and wit.

'So, have you spoken to Joe?' Lawrence asked Max.

'No, why?'

'Him and Gina have split up,' Lawrence announced, downing the last of his lager.

'No, I haven't seen him in a couple of days. Is he okay?'

I loved the way Max asked if Joe was okay, not Gina. I hoped she was, but I didn't want Max worrying about her emotional state.

'Think so. Apparently, she said it was all happening too quick. I mean, come on, four months and getting married? Bit quick, if you ask me.'

Lawrence didn't know about our baby; Max decided he wanted to wait until the scan was over. I wondered what Lawrence would say about us when he found out.

The slow music was enticing others to join the happy couple but my feet and back were killing me and I couldn't think of anything worse than dancing. Lawrence had other plans as he asked Suzy to join him. He was much taller than Suzy but they looked really good together. I commented to Max how this could be a new-found affair. We watched as they laughed, Suzy obviously enjoying his company very much. This was definitely going somewhere.

'So, I was thinking.' Max pulled me towards him. We hugged on the chairs like a drunken couple, although I'd not touched a drop after the champagne that morning, as it had sent a wave of nausea through me.

'What were you thinking?'

'Well, we should get married.'

'What?' I sat up to face him. 'Was that a proposal?'

'It was a bit crap, wasn't it?'

'I'll say.' I smiled at his cheeky grin. 'Look, let's have our baby and then talk marriage or whatever in a few years.'

'Okay, you're right,' he agreed.

It wasn't that I didn't want to get married. I did, eventually. But we had so many other things going on, I didn't want to organise a wedding at the moment. I cuddled back into him. 'So, what do you think about Joe and Gina?' I asked, casually.

'What are you getting at?'

'Nothing, I was just asking.' My unconcerned approach hadn't worked.

'I don't think anything. Please let's not go into this again. We should be happy. This is a happy time for us. I chose you, so you—'

'You chose me?' I asked, sitting back up again.

He swallowed hard, obviously realising what he'd said. He tried to backtrack and said, 'You know what I mean.'

But I didn't.

'Christ. I can't believe I've drunk too much and blurted this stuff out,' he said.

'Get on with it, Max.'

'When I first came into the salon—'

'You were still with her?'

'No. No.' He shook his head, trying to get his drunken brain around sober words. 'We hadn't been split up that long.'

'How long?' I realised I'd never asked.

'About a month, but we'd been out for a meal to see if we could work it out. We were still sort-of talking about getting back together.'

'You're kidding me?' I felt as if he'd been cheating but I knew he hadn't.

'Look, nothing happened. I promise on our baby's life that nothing happened once you and I were together. I never really saw her again after our first date. I told her I'd met someone else and she was happy with that.'

'Do you think she dated Joe to make you jealous?' I asked, feeling settled that there had been nothing going on between them. He didn't have to come back to the salon, but he had.

'I don't know and I don't care. I love you. I want you. Let's get married.'

I hit him playfully, then cuddled into him and watched Suzy and Lawrence joking and laughing with each other.

'I do love you, Kat, you do know that, don't you?' Max said seriously, although he was slurring slightly. His eyes were locked into mine.

'I love you too.' I said.

I meant it. I truly felt complete.

35

We sat with our blue bag, given to us by Pam on her first midwife visit. I felt quite big, for someone one who was having a twelve-week scan. Well, if our dates were right, I was actually about fourteen weeks now. I looked pregnant. Well, I thought I did. It only took a slim-fitting T-shirt to make me look six months; either that or I looked like I'd been eating too many pies.

No one else in the waiting room looked pregnant. There were no obvious bumps, whereas I looked as if I was coming for a twenty-week scan. I hid my bump with a long cardigan, the one I'd bought during the adventure of buying the pregnancy-testing kit. I'd never actually worn it before now. It wasn't my favourite but it was one of the biggest, and discreetly covered the weight gain. Admittedly, as I covered my bloated stomach I realised I'd never thought about my weight much until I arrived here.

I was bursting for the toilet. The scan letter had advised a full bladder. Mine couldn't be any fuller than it was now. Suzy had emphasised the importance of this, something to do with a full bladder changing the position of the uterus, pushing it up so it was easier to scan. Another piece of information she'd collected from all those magazines. Most women had their partners with them, others sat with older women who I assumed were their mothers. I tried to imagine having Marianne here. It made me smile, because she would probably have been the next one in line, if Max for whatever reason couldn't have made it. I'd even contemplated having Clare with me as she had become so considerate. She still had her overpowering and controlling ways, but they were easier to handle when she was being a nice person.

As we sat waiting for our scan, I felt as if life was venturing down a path which I would never have chosen, but embracing it was enabling me to look forward to the journey ahead. Don't get me wrong, I was full of anticipation; but there was a glimmer of light which wasn't on my radar when Suzy and I had done the test.

'Kathryn Neasham,' an older nurse shouted, almost as if I was a criminal. Max and I rose from our seats quickly. I hoped she wasn't doing the scan, she seemed so brisk. We walked towards the small room, nerves fluttering in my stomach. A formal hospital bed stood covered in a roll of blue paper. Next to the bed stood a huge machine, which looked colossal and unnecessary. Luckily, a younger (I'm not being ageist), more pleasant woman greeted us.

'Right, my love, if you get comfortable on the bed,' she told me. As I did so, she explained she was called Linda, she was a sonographer and that we would be checking a few things with the baby today. She asked me to lift my top and undo the top buttons on my jeans, as the scan needed to be further down towards the womb so we could see the baby. Max and I were quiet; both of us tense with anticipation. It was the strange, unknown surroundings which sparked my anxiety. I was eager for the first glimpse of our baby. I'd read a few magazines, seen a few pictures, but I wasn't sure what to expect. Would we be able to see anything?

Linda rubbed wet gel across my stomach, which felt disgusting, but I didn't say so. She said she would have a good look around first, then Max and I could have a look. We both nodded, not daring to speak. Max was sitting behind her, watching the screen, his blank expression indicating he couldn't figure out what she was looking at. Linda seemed extremely focused on the screen.

She pushed the scanner on to the gel, her firmness making me concentrate hard on controlling my bladder, in case I peed myself mid-scan.

She roamed about with the machine, pushing it down in some areas, pressing buttons on her keyboard. Max's eyes were wide as he took in whatever it was Linda was viewing. She frowned and nodded but gave me no indication whether everything was okay. Five minutes later, she smiled and turned the screen to face me.

'Well, both heartbeats are doing well.'

'You can see mine on there?' I wasn't surprised because it felt as if it was bursting out of my chest.

'Erm …' Linda bit her lip. Her eyes met mine as she smiled warily.

'No. You're having twins.'

'Twins?' Max and I stared at each other. A little bit of wee came out as I gasped for breath. Twins?

I thought my life had become chaos; I think the chaos was just about to begin.

-THE END-

A Note from Bombshell Books

Thanks for reading Holding Myself. We hope you enjoyed it as much as we did. Please consider leaving a review on Amazon or Goodreads to help others find and enjoy this book too.

We make every effort to ensure that books are carefully edited and proofread, however occasionally mistakes do slip through. If you spot something, please do send details to info@ bombshellbooks.com and we can amend it.

Bombshell Books specialise in women's fiction. We regularly have special offers including free and discounted eBooks. To be the first to hear about these special offers, why not join our mailing list here? We won't send you more than two emails per month and we'll never pass your details on to anybody else.

Readers who enjoyed Holding Myself will also enjoy

The Queen Of Blogging by Therese Loreskar.

Acknowledgements

Thank you to Simon, Alexia and Gabriella. My gorgeous family. I am truly blessed. You are my world.

An enormous thank you to all my family and friends, who have not only supported me in my writing dreams but encouraged me to move forward and reach my goals. I feel extremely lucky and I'm so grateful for having such special people in my life.

Massive thank you to Karen Pickering and KA Richardson for being my extra pair of eyes when I first initially put these stories together. Your help was appreciated more than you know.

A special thank you to the late, Jenny Drewery, my first amazing editor, for her amazing support and invaluable guidance, you were an inspiration.

Last, but definitely not least, a massive thank you to Betsy and all the hard-working team at Bombshell Books, I am truly thankful for your belief in me, and helping to make my dreams come true.